Bat Boy

�042

UKA PRESS PUBLISHING

Offices in the UK, Europe and Japan
Olympiaweg 102-hs, 1076 XG, Amsterdam, The Netherlands
St.A., 108, 2-5-22 Shida, Fujieda, Shizuoka 426-0071, Japan

2 4 6 8 10 9 7 5 3 1

First published in Great Britain in 2011 by UKA Press

ISBN: 978-1-905796-25-0

Eiting, Cover & Interior Design by D. Masters, St. A, UKA Press

Printed and Bound in Great Britain and the USA

Bat Boy

by

Chris Barraclough

UKA PRESS PUBLISHING

For Victoria – Love you forever, LWT

Part One... How it Happened

One

On the morning it happened, Saturday the 22nd of December, I woke up at seven a.m. exactly. Even though I don't do school like other kids, I still like to get up early every day so I have time to walk Chops, our Doberman Pinscher, before I start on the day's studies. Chops is Pat's dog really, but because Pat is so busy working most of the time, it's up to me to look after him. I don't mind at all though, because he's a really great dog.

The only problem with Chops is he can seem a little fierce if you don't know him, because he really likes to bark at things. He barks at people, he barks at other dogs, he barks at trees, rocks, lamp posts and post boxes. He barks at the television a lot, especially when Jeremy Kyle is on. Most people think he's 'simple', but Pat once put it like this:

"Humans are all different, right? Some are all kind and friendly and stuff, like those Jehova's wotsits, and some are total dicks, like…I dunno, Osama Bin Laden. And dogs are the same, eh? Some are all quiet and obedient and fetching you the paper types, and then some are just total bastards who don't care what anyone thinks, like Chops."

I frowned. "Are you saying our dog is like Osama Bin Laden?"

"Well, I'm not saying he's gonna become a radical dog terrorist and start taking corgis hostage. Just that compared to other dogs, he's a bit of a prick."

I don't agree with Pat – I once read that Dobermans as a breed are fairly temperamental, and get agitated around anyone they see as a rival. So Chops must see rocks, lamp posts and Jeremy Kyle as great rivals.

After I showered and dressed, I got my books ready for morning studies then headed down the hallway.

The house was still silent, aside from the occasional grunt or snort from Mum's bedroom, and the endless ticking from the cheap Swiss clock in the lounge. I crept down the stairs, the worn fabric tickling between my toes, and turned right into the kitchen. This morning it smelled of tuna and marmite – Pat's favourite sandwich combination.

As usual, I edged my hand across the end of the narrow breakfast table, which was covered in sand-like bread crumbs. Two empty wine bottles were lined up beside the bowl of mushy fruit. Last night must have been a bad one.

The soft *pip pap pip pap* of Chops' feet across the tiled floor announced his imminent arrival, along with the usual heavy panting and his familiar scent – he always seemed to have that wet-dog smell, even when he was completely dry. Chops' head pushed against the back of my leg, and I reached down and scratched him behind the ears, just the way he likes. Unfortunately, like most things in life, this provoked an assault of excited barks.

"Shush boy!" I hissed, "you'll wake Mum! She'll be really pissed off!"

But my desperate pleading had no effect, so I ran to the corner of the room and unhooked his leash from the back door.

"Come on, then, let's get out of here."

After I slipped on my trainers and hooked the leash to his collar, I opened the door and let Chops rush past. Luckily I had a tight hold on the end of the leash, or else he would have been off down the street by himself, chasing the first thing that dared to move. I just about managed to hold him back long enough to get the door closed behind me. I paused only to listen for any kind of sound from upstairs – but the house had fallen silent again.

For December the air was surprisingly warm, enough to wear my jacket open and discard the gloves and hat, so I decided to take Chops to the park where he could charge about and get some exercise. He loved aimlessly running around almost as much as he loved barking. We walked over to our usual quiet spot at the near end of the park, just across the track and through a narrow band of trees. Chops pulled against the leash so hard that he started to wheeze, so I let him loose. Like a cannonball he was away. His paws scrambled through the grass and his frantic panting quickly faded into the distance.

After he galloped off across the field, I collapsed to the soft ground and lay back, my head nestled in my hands and my legs stretched out. The grass was still cold, the damp tips tickling the nape of my neck. I shuffled until I got comfortable, then lay still, breathing in the delicious scent of chopped grass while the winter sun warmed my face.

Somewhere just beyond the trees I heard a boy and his father. The pair laughed and clapped over the drone of a propeller that must have belonged to some kind of remote-controlled plane. They may have been having fun, but not as much fun as Chops, who had already found a victim to bark at and pursued his sport with great enthusiasm.

I focused on his overexcited yaps for a while, making sure he didn't stray too far, but the reassuring touch of the sun and the soothing breeze soon caused my concentration to drift. I finally lost track of him and slipped into a blissful sleep.

How long I was out for, I have no idea.

The next thing I remember, I was sat bolt upright. My chest heaved uncontrollably. The warm glow from the sun had departed and the air had regained its chilly edge, even though the breeze was absent. But what really freaked me was the silence. There wasn't a sound for miles around, aside from my own desperate breathing and the assault of my heart against my ribcage. The laughter of the boy and his father was gone. All around, no other people walking or talking, no jets flying overhead or birds squawking.

More importantly, I couldn't hear Chops barking or panting or tearing about the field.

"Chops?" I called out.

I paused for any kind of response. None came.

I clambered to my feet and called again, but still there was nothing but creepy silence.

My back dripped with sweat. My skin was clammy and cold. I shivered and wrapped my arms across my chest to squeeze myself tight.

Strange thoughts forced themselves to the surface of my mind, thoughts about what could have happened while I was sleeping. Maybe the world's population had been wiped out by some new kind of virus, a mutated airborne disease inhaled by its victims, or some terrible pathogen transmitted by killer monkeys – it was always killer monkeys. Once inside a person's body, it systematically dissolved every cell in a matter of minutes, until all that remained was a puddle of blood and dust. Or perhaps it was some global catastrophe, a worldwide terrorist attack, or an alien invasion, and for some reason I had been left untouched, the last remaining human on Earth. My lower lip shook and I cried out for Chops until my throat was hoarse, but it did no good. He was nowhere around.

That was when I heard something shuffle in the grass, 20 yards to my right. Every muscle in my body turned to rock.

"Who's there?" I called, my voice paper-thin. No reply, and the shuffling stopped.

I could tell now that it was another person – a heavy-set man, from his strained gasps. He must have been holding his breath before, so I couldn't hear him. A sharp pang rippled through my stomach. I would've given anything right then to hear Chops bark and thump his way towards me across the grass. But we were alone. Just me and the stranger, together in the middle of the deserted park.

I wanted so badly to run but my legs were locked in place, as if someone had nailed my feet to the floor or tied blocks of lead around my ankles. The rest of my body could only tremble. For a moment all I could focus on was the icy drops of sweat that soaked into my shirt and the biting chill of the air against my skin. But then a tinny and muffled strain of a familiar song burst into life from the stranger's direction. It was Mozart's Symphony Number 25, and it must have come from his mobile phone.

The haunting notes somehow snapped me from my stupor, and I twisted and tore across the field away from him.

He yelled something, his words lost to the wind, then his footsteps pounded across the ground behind me. The air whipped past my face and swept away my tears, but I barely felt its cold pinch. Instead, I desperately tried to work out how far it was to the thin strip of oaks ahead. We had walked 165 paces past the trees, but with greater strides it would only be half of that before I reached them again. I counted down each step as best I could, but I was so terrified that the numbers were a blur.

My legs burned, my nose and throat clogged with snot and spit. But the stranger kept pace behind me and I didn't dare slow. I imagined him with a hunting knife clutched in his fist, the blade stained with the dried blood of his victims. A croaky yelp escaped my lips. Could he have murdered every other person in the park, only to leave me for last? What if I tripped over the remains of the father and son who had moments ago been laughing and playing? Their entrails could still be spread across the grass somewhere up ahead. Just one wrong step and I would slip on a shredded pancreas, and the stranger would claim his final victim.

The grass suddenly turned to a crisp layer of dried leaves that crunched beneath my feet, and the thud of each step was echoed back at me. I was almost at the trees. I stretched my arms out to protect myself, too terrified to slow even with the thick trunks that loomed ahead. After only a few more steps, my left elbow slammed into something solid. The blow spun me around and almost knocked me to the ground. As I cried out, my arms flailed at my sides. Somehow I managed to stay on my feet, but the collision had been enough for the stranger to catch up.

Pudgy fingers wrapped around my wrist and the stranger's pungent breath washed over my face, bitter and stale. Even that stink was overpowered by the terrible reek of his aftershave, which stung me to the very back of my throat. Immediately I threw my foot out and the tip of my boot connected with something solid. The stranger's pants turned to a strangled cry, then his grip on my arm weakened. This was it! My chance to escape!

I pulled back and his sweat-drenched fingers slipped from my skin, but I lost my balance and stumbled backwards through the leaves. My right hand shot out and clawed at something rough. I grabbed a handful of what felt like jagged bark, which splintered and dug under my nails. It was just enough to twist me back around. I sprinted forwards again, away from the stranger.

Finally I emerged from the trees, despite almost cracking my ankles on jutting roots or slipping on pools of moss and mud.

As soon as the firm ground returned, I pounded my legs as hard as I could. My muscles burned as if they'd wrenched themselves apart and were clinging to my bones with tendril fingers. Trails of snot and bubbling tears streaked across my face, but it was a distant sensation, barely noticeable. For the first time I could remember, the darkness that surrounded me felt as if it was going to swallow me whole. There was no escape from the heavy-set man. He'd chase me down until I had no more strength and collapsed to the ground, a shivering wreck, and then he would take his time carving me into tiny pieces, no bigger than a fun-size Mars Bar.

Every breath I sucked in caused my chest to shudder. The agony in my lungs was unbearable, as if I was inhaling toxic gas. My legs powered me forwards through no will of my own, guided by some malevolent force.

The road was close. I could already hear the drone of cars up ahead, and the sound spurred me on.

At last I made it. My feet slapped against the gravel pavement that ran alongside the road at the end of the park, and I crumpled up. My hands clutched my trembling knees while a wave of nausea clenched my stomach into a ball. For a minute I rested, streams of spit gushing from my lower lip. I was safe here – or so I hoped.

A steady flow of cars sped past just a few feet away, the passengers all potential witnesses or rescuers if the stranger was still in pursuit. I stood there until my breath returned and the nausea passed. Still no footsteps behind me. I was alone again.

A fresh wall of tears built up behind my eyes and I wiped my face with the back of my hand. I didn't know if it was because I was scared, or angry, or maybe just relieved, but I began to sob. My fingers desperately swept away the drops that poured down my cheeks and over my quivering lips, while the sound of Chops' frantic barking echoed around my skull as if he stood right beside me. I felt his head brush against my legs to reassure me everything would be okay, but when I reached down to pat him, my fingers could not find him. Had the stranger harmed him, or even…no, why would anyone do that? He was just a damn harmless dog, and I loved him so much.

Now I wailed in fury, my hands balled into fists at my sides. I wanted to turn around and run straight back into the park, to hunt across every last acre until I found my dog, even though the stranger still lurked there. Instead, I just stood in place and cried in helpless self-pity.

The tears had formed a sticky second skin over my cheeks when I heard a car pull up next to me. The engine growled like a cornered fox. I sniffed and took a step backwards, and my heart raced once more as a window hummed open.

"Hey, you okay, kid?" asked a middle-aged lady.

From the rasp of her voice, she must have smoked more than Winston Churchill. I just nodded, my mind suddenly blank, then I took off down the pavement despite the weariness that soaked through my limbs. My feet kicked up showers of gravel the whole way.

The pavement stretched on for just under half a mile, and I half-ran, half-staggered the entire length. At the end, I turned off and bounded up the concrete steps that led up the steep embankment to our house. The gate was open a crack when I arrived and I barged straight through it without pausing to close it again. It took me three attempts to get my key in the door because my hand trembled so much. When it finally clicked into place, I shouldered the door aside, stumbled into the kitchen, and collapsed knees-first onto the icy tiles.

As soon as I slammed the door shut, I slumped back against it and dug my nails into the surface. That sound? The gate – did it just slam shut again? My fingers flew at the latch and twisted it until it clicked. I could almost feel the hot breath on the back of my neck, smell the pungent stench of his aftershave again. My back, clammy and stiff, slid down the door. My arse hit the ground and I curled up right there, completely spent.

I don't know how long I lay there for, with my knees crushed into my chest and my arms wrapped tight around my legs, but that was how Mum found me. The sound of her footsteps on the stairs stirred me. I was too exhausted to pull myself to my feet, as if all of my strength had poured from my body and trickled into the narrow cracks in the floor. She came into the kitchen and stopped suddenly, her breath caught in her chest. Then she sighed, mumbled something, and padded across to the breakfast table in her worn old slippers with the loose slapping soles. Each step sounded like a tremendous effort. Her feet slapped and pounded into the tiles as if she carried an armful of boulders.

A clink of glass was followed by a crash and more mumbling.

"Hell's wrong with you?" she said.

I sniffed and shook my head. My throat was crushed shut, my lungs nothing more than useless, soggy bags. How I longed to be somewhere far away from every other person on Earth, in the middle of a steamy jungle or an endless stretching desert, or – even better – drifting out in the emptiness of space, in a one-man pod. Surviving on dried pineapple ice cream.

"Well, you're going to just sit there all damn day?"

"Chops is gone," I said, although the words came out as nothing more than a petrified croak.

"What did you say? Speak up! You're blind, not dumb, aren't you!"

"I said Chops, Chops is gone!"

She must have heard me this time because she stopped what she was doing. Next, I heard her slippers slap towards me. Her hand grabbed me just above my elbow and she yanked me from the floor, and the force of it wrenched my arm in the socket. The pain was horrific, as if splinters of barbed wire had sliced their way through my shoulder.

I cried out, but it was a mistake to cry or complain – that always got her started. Her fingers dug even further into my arm and her nails cut through the thin material of my t-shirt and clawed at my skin.

"What do you mean, he's gone? What did you do, Joel?"

"I just took him to the park," I said. I tried to pull her hand away, but her grip was a vice. "I fell asleep, and when I woke up he was just gone! Then…" I swallowed and sucked in a breath. "Then someone tried to grab me, so I had to run."

"You stupid child!" She shook me, and my head whipped back and forth, almost snapped clean off my shoulders. This time I didn't cry. I receded as far back into the depths of my mind as I could manage, a trick I'd managed many times and had near-perfected. So far down, until all of this was just a fuzzy dream, nothing more.

"I've told you not to let him off his leash, haven't I? Why don't you ever listen to me!"

She gave me another shake, then a tremendous shove that sent me flying backwards.

I screamed as something sharp slammed into the back of my skull and gashed through my scalp. The next thing I knew, I was sprawled across the floor, my cheek pressed against a cold kitchen tile. I felt a stream of bile trickle up my throat but quickly swallowed it back. Thoughts blurred.

Mum slammed the cupboard door and I heard her footsteps slap out of the kitchen.

A hot trickle of blood seeped through my hair from the gash, and my shoulder throbbed, in time with my heartbeat, *it hurts, Mum, it hurts bad.*

For a while I lay there trembling and gasping, concentrating on the pain, willing it away, until finally it started to ease off. I reached for the table leg, gripped it, and managed to haul myself up from the floor. Then I held my breath, listening for Chops. But there was no sound from outside. The only noise in the entire house – besides the constant ticking of the Swiss clock – was the muffled screech of the television upstairs.

Two

For the rest of the day until Pat returned home, I sat alone in my room and contemplated life. I thought about what I had done. Whether I really was a bad or stupid person. I wondered who the stranger was, and what he had done to Chops. Once or twice (actually, six times in all), I crept downstairs and made my way to the back door, where I softly slid it open, hoping to be greeted by a friendly bark. All six times I was met only with the sound of the gate as it slammed shut, caught in the growing gale.

When I finally heard Pat's key scrape in the lock downstairs, my stomach almost ejected itself out of my mouth.

I sat and waited on my bed while he grabbed some juice from the fridge and made his way up.

He passed by my door and nudged open his own. Next came the familiar thud of his rucksack being hurled against the wardrobe, before his footsteps trudged back down the hallway. This was followed by the usual three sharp knocks. My door creaked open.

"Hey man, how come it's so quiet in here?" He closed the door and sat beside me. "What's up? You look like crap. Hey, you haven't been crying, have ya?"

"It's Chops. I lost him in the park."

I sucked in a deep breath and relived those terrible moments for the hundredth time. By now, the memories really did seem like some terrible dream.

"What, he ran off?"

"I don't know. I lay down for a bit, and I must have dozed off, and when I woke up again I couldn't hear him. But then there was this man standing right next to me, and he didn't say anything when I asked who he was, and I was so scared that I just ran. He chased after me, almost got me. I thought he was going to kidnap me, or kill me or something."

"Bloody hell, Joel! Did you tell Mum all this?"

"I tried to." I sunk my head and buried my face in my palms, which were still hot and soaked with sweat.

"Oh man, you're bleeding!" I felt his fingers part my hair just behind my right ear. "Did that tosser in the park do this?"

"No. I just fell, in the kitchen."

In the brief moment of silence I wondered why I had lied, and considered confessing. Before I had the chance, he stood and pulled me to my feet.

"C'mon, we gotta wash that, before it gets infected."

I held my head over the bathroom sink while Pat splashed hot, soapy water onto the cut. It stung pretty bad, but the gasp I let out was nothing compared to my screams when he doused the whole wound with antiseptic.

"Hold still, ya wimp." He gripped my skull with one hand. "Stop shaking, will ya? You'll only have yourself to blame if it turns all green and minging, and your head falls off."

He dried me, then wrapped a bandage around my head and pinned it in place. The bandage felt kind of strange and uncomfortable, but he assured me that it made me look like a right little Rambo. Although his remarks didn't help me feel any better, I still managed a weak smile.

"Thanks, Pat."

"No worries. Come on, Rambowski, you wanna head to the park and look for Chops?"

I nodded. Any hopes I had of finding him again had practically crumbled, but I had to go out and search for him, and with Pat here I at least felt safe again. We pulled on our coats.

The sound of the television still drifted from Mum's room as we headed downstairs. I was thankful that her door stayed closed while we left.

A bitter wind had risen by the time we arrived at the park, and the reassuring touch of the sun had already vanished. We took the embankment in huge strides to try and stay warm. I led Pat to the exact spot where I had laid down that morning, through the trees where the stranger had grabbed me and then straight across to the middle of the park. The entire field was as eerily silent as before.

"Can't see him around," Pat said. He made no remarks about seeing mutilated corpses or disembodied pancreases, which was some little relief.

"Chops took off over there when I let him off the leash." I pointed in the direction that I'd heard him gallop, away from the trees. "He never usually goes far, though."

"Maybe he was chasing summat. Duck, or a goose, summat like that. Over there's the lake, the dumb mutt could've jumped right in."

We continued towards the lake and took up a position on the bank, near a lone duck. We must have freaked it, because it quacked and flapped its wings at us, sending tiny gusts that caught against my cheek.

I wondered if Chops had chased the duck earlier. If so, that would probably explain its agitation. I carefully edged away.

"Can you see him anywhere?"

"Nah, but I can't really see into the lake. It's too dark."

"But if he did fall in there, he'd be able to swim to the edge, right?"

"I dunno, can dogs swim?"

"Yeah, I'm pretty sure they can. They named a whole swimming style after them."

"What, doggy style?"

"Doggy paddle, not doggy style."

I dropped onto the damp grass and crossed my legs, then clutched my head in my hands and rubbed my temples with cold fingertips.

The thought that Chops could be floating somewhere in there, down in that freezing cold water, made my guts churn. If he really was dead, it would all be my fault. My eyes stung and I dabbed at them with my sleeve. I hoped so bad that he had just run off, and was happily chasing ducks, or geese, or some other unsuspecting wildlife on the other side of the park.

I wished I could somehow go back in time to this morning and stop myself from ever leaving the house. I wished none of this had ever happened and I was sat home right now, eating pizza and playing with Pat and Chops. While I was at it, I wished, as usual, for a million pounds, and the power of sight, and my own desert island, and a plane so I could stock up on ice cream and pizza any time I needed.

"It's okay, we'll find him."

Pat slumped down next to me and slapped me on the back. The blow knocked me from my thoughts. "Cheer up, Joel. He's pretty dumb, but I don't think he'd jump in the lake, the big wuss. Bet he'll be back at the house already."

"Can we just look a little longer?"

"Well, all right then. Let's head back down the edge of the forest. Keep your ears peeled, right?"

We walked in a broad semi-circle alongside the tall oaks, where the grass became patchy, flattened by the constant joggers. Occasionally I heard a rustle or a scratching sound from amongst the trees, but it was always smaller creatures, never heavy or lumbering enough to be Chops.

The wind prickled my skin right through my jacket, and my ears throbbed so bad from the chill that it felt as if tiny bugs had burrowed into my brain. Still, I couldn't bear to head back just yet.

Finally, after we'd walked the entire edge of the forest, Pat said, "Come on, we ain't gonna find him out here tonight. I can't see a damn thing, it's too dark."

"But what if he needs our help?"

My voice broke apart, my throat all dry and tender. I pushed the button on the side of my watch.

"Six fifteen pee em," said the emotionless female voice, who sounded a lot like a cyborg version of Judi Dench. I hated that voice, but Pat had bought me the watch for my tenth birthday with some money he had saved up, and I didn't have the heart to tell him. It wasn't all that bad, to be honest – it kept good time at least – but the voice creeped me out. A lot.

"It's only early still, can't we just check around the playground?"

"Nah, we better head back. Mum'll kill us if she finds out we were hanging round here after dark."

"I bet she wouldn't care at all," I muttered, my lower lip stuck out. My remark was met with silence.

"C'mon," Pat eventually said, "let's get back. I'll cook us some pizza, eh? I don't have to start work till noonish tomorrow, so we can look for him in the morning. Maybe stick up some posters or summat."

"Okay," I said, my head lowered. I felt Pat's arm across my neck and we changed direction. "Do you really think we'll ever see him again?"

"Course we will, don't worry about it. You wanna play some Mortal Kombat when we get back, while the pizza cooks?" Again I nodded. "I might even let you win," Pat said, squeezing my shoulder. I smiled and elbowed him in the ribs. He knew only too well that I'd crush him as usual, even without the ability to actually see the screen. All I had to do was bust out Scorpion's harpoon move and he was finished.

We pushed our way through the trees and emerged into the sloping field, where a fearsome gust of wind almost swept us both off our feet. We broke into a jog, the silence broken by our whoops and howls. The gale practically carried us down the slope, but by the time we reached the side of the road it had died down. We slowed to a brisk pace.

"So you sprinted all the way back through the park?" Pat asked between pants. "Without Chops to guide you or anything?"

"Yeah. I was pretty freaked out by that guy."

"You must have been. Jeez, you really are a Bat Boy, eh?"

"Don't call me that, you know I hate it."

"That's why I do it," Pat replied, and I could tell that his lips were twisted into his usual toothy grin. I sighed and shook my head. Rambowski was probably a better name, I thought. It made me sound tough, confident, kind of cool. Anyway, anything but Bat Boy.

He'd used that name ever since I was seven and he was nine, when we'd stayed with Uncle Bill for a few months up in Scotland. Uncle Bill lived right on the Northern coast, in the middle of absolutely nowhere. In fact, the one road that led to within a mile of his house was so narrow that it didn't even appear on a Scottish A-to-Z. Mostly because no one in their right mind would ever actually venture out there, even by accident.

The only real company we had was an albatross that lived on one of the crags, a big brute that would squawk to itself for hours on end. Our uncle wasn't much fun to be around. All he ever did was smoke, sleep, and occasionally drive the 50-mile round trip to the nearest store to pick up meat, beans and coal.

And so we explored in our masses of spare time. We trekked high over hills and deep into valleys in the hope of finding adventure – or at least some quiet away from the bloody albatross.

One day we wandered a little further up the beach than usual, and came across a cave that sank deep into the side of the cliffs.

Pat was so excited that he left me there while he ran back to grab our uncle's torch. As soon as he returned we wandered in. The cave quickly narrowed into a tunnel, which seemed to dip down into the earth.

The place grew cooler and damper the further we stalked, and freezing cold water droplets rained down and soaked us the whole way. I soon wanted to turn back, but Pat was desperate to explore further. He was convinced we'd discover a lost civilisation or piles of pirate treasure, or maybe even a genie who'd grant us wishes. If we really had found a genie, my first wish would have been to get us well out of Scotland.

Unfortunately, just 20 minutes later – after he'd led us down various passages and tunnels – he realised we were completely, utterly lost. All thoughts of cave people and magical genies vanished, and panic set in.

We started back, but quickly came to a junction of three different tunnels. Pat had no idea which one we'd come from. He shouted and stomped his feet and complained that we'd be trapped in there forever, forced to live off moss and insects – which actually didn't seem too bad, compared to Uncle Bill's cooking. Once he'd finished his hysterical outburst, I grabbed his arm and led him straight down the middle path, and from there we twisted and turned our way through the cavernous maze.

For most of the journey he insisted that I was getting us even more lost, but finally his tone changed from terrified to ecstatic, and he shouted that he could see daylight up ahead.

Moments later, we emerged back out onto the beach. All I'd done was retrace our steps, which I could remember perfectly, but Pat was convinced from that point that I had some sort of psychic power, or sixth sense.

And that's how I got the nickname 'Bat Boy'. The invincible, all-seeing, magical bat-vision Bat Boy.

"I really thought that guy was going to hurt me," I said. I kicked my foot through the gravel, carving a trench in the pebbles. "Why else would he try and grab me right in the middle of a park?"

"It was probably some drunken old tramp. You see a few of them hanging 'round back there sometimes."

"A tramp with a mobile phone?"

"Could've nicked it, maybe. Summat to sell, get some cash for a bottle of white lightning, or some crystal meth. Tramps love crystal meth. Anyways, I couldn't see anyone about there tonight, so whoever it was must've buggered off. You better not go there on your own though, just in case, right? We'll go looking for Chops together tomorrow, yeah?"

"Yeah, okay."

"Ahh, it's funny, like."

"What's funny? Sinister men trying to kidnap me?"

"Nah, the fact you ran all the way back home no worries, but cracked yer head good an' proper on the kitchen floor when you got back. Daft sod. How's it feeling?"

"Still throbbing." That familiar feeling returned in the centre of my stomach, the dull ache that swiftly spread throughout my entire gut. My feet kicked against each other and I almost tripped, but Pat stopped me before I tumbled helplessly to the ground.

"Hey, Joel, crap, y'okay? Joel?"

"I don't want to go home," I whispered. I buried my face against his shoulder and sucked in the scent of old sweat and smoke.

Pat grabbed my arms and pulled me back, his fingers digging into me.

"What's wrong with you?"

"I…" I wanted so badly to tell him what had happened, but something held me back. Maybe deep in my heart I knew what would happen if I did.

Fresh tears sprang from my eyes and ran down my cheeks, and I couldn't tell if Pat was concerned or simply appalled at the sight of me.

"What's up, man? Why ya crying?"

"I didn't fall over in the kitchen. It was Mum. She pushed me." The words came out just like that, almost by accident, as if my mouth had blabbed all by itself. Almost immediately I regretted it, although right then I had no idea how those words would change our lives.

"Mum pushed you?"

I could hear his breath tighten into sharp, angry little bursts. His grip tightened until his fingers crushed my arms, and it wasn't until I wriggled and moaned that he finally let go. He turned and strode across the gravel, only for a few steps, then he let out a tremendous roar. Chunks of rock scattered clear across the road.

"That drunken bitch, I'll do her in!"

"Pat," I said, and I took a step towards him. "Pat, I'm sorry, I didn't want to tell you. Please, Pat."

I pleaded, begged for him to forget what I had said. But I knew it was already too late.

"Why'd you not want to tell me? So she can do it again, and again? She done this to you before?"

"No, I swear! I don't think she meant it, it was just an accident. She was upset about Chops, and it's my fault that he's missing, anyway."

"Don't ever make excuses for her! What's she thinking, picking on someone who can't even…I don't care when she does it to me, but – and she just left you there, bleeding, right?"

Another explosion of rocks, and a car blared its horn as it roared past.

"She's a mess, Joel. I dunno why we put up with it. If it weren't for the money she gets for us, she'd have no money, no food. No bloody wine. We should've had her taken away years ago."

"Please don't tell her I told you," I said, and I reached out and grabbed hold of his coat. "Please, Pat."

"No way. I ain't letting her get away with this." I knew from the tone of his voice that he wasn't going to change his mind.

••
Three

Pat shoved the back door open and his boots slammed across the kitchen as if he was trying to smash the tiles. I followed him inside, paused to close the door, then ran after him.

I had no chance keeping up with Pat on the stairs. He stomped into Mum's room before I was halfway up. The television blared through the open door and I could make out the excited chatter of some American sit-com stars, and laughter from a studio audience. I stopped on the stairs and stood still, holding my breath as if that would make me invisible. My fingers tightened around the banister. I thought back to the last confrontation, and the night we'd spent in the shed afterwards, arms wrapped tight around each other as we sat shivering on a tattered blanket, shying away from the freezing gusts that seeped in through the cracks.

The laughter from the television was suddenly cut off. "What the hell are you doing? Turn it back on!"

"Or what?" Pat yelled. "You'll thump me?"

"I'll rake your bloody eyes out!" She slurred her words, same as always around this time in the evening. I heard her struggle to climb from her seat, the wooden frame creaking and groaning. Something heavy dropped to the floor. Whatever it was bounced once on the shaggy carpet.

"Now look what you made me do! Bloody hell!"

"I've put up with your abuse for years, Mum, but I ain't gonna watch you put Joel through the same thing. You keep your hands off him, or I report you, right?"

"Oh, so that's what it's all about? Spreading lies, same as always, that devious little – as if I would hit him! Did he tell you he lost the dog?"

"He said you pushed him. His head's gashed right open!"

"I never laid a hand on him! What bloody lies! Get him in here." I heard the chair creak. "I'll get the truth out of him!"

My face began to burn and sickness crept through my entire body. My legs felt heavy and useless, buckling beneath me. If I hadn't been clutching the banister, I would probably have collapsed and tumbled to the bottom like a sack of rocks.

"You're pathetic, Mum! What the hell do you ever do, eh? You just sit here drinking and watching that box!"

"You selfish little bastards, I've given you everything! If it wasn't for me, you wouldn't even be here!"

"That's your whole idea of being a mother, ain't it? Spit us out and then let us fend for ourselves! If it wasn't for my job, the two of us would have nowt!"

I silently begged them to stop, but even if I'd called out, my voice would have been only a whisper. The creaking came again as Mum struggled again to stand up. This time her seat snapped back and I heard her feet stomp unevenly across the rumpled carpet. The ear-crunching tones of the Americans rang out again. Pat raised his voice, and Mum screamed back.

Finally I had to move. I was to blame for what had happened. If I didn't go in there and speak for myself – if I let Pat fight my battle for me like so many times before – I'd be the worst kind of coward.

My feet shuffled forwards. Inch by inch I crept towards the screaming, until a terrifying crash echoed from the bedroom. I stopped dead, my teeth clenched. Maybe being a coward wasn't so bad after all. I took a step back.

"He's just as bloody thick as you are!" Mum screamed, her voice strained as if she'd shouted herself hoarse.

"No, he's not! He's really bright, no thanks to you, and he's gonna show you how smart he is as soon as he gets outta this hole!"

I groaned and slid a foot forwards again. As terrified as I was, I couldn't leave him alone in there. He was only half the size of Mum.

When I finally reached the room, I stood in the doorway and grabbed the wooden frame on either side. The screams suddenly died. I could tell their eyes were locked on me.

"I'm sorry," was all I could say. I didn't even know what I was apologising for any more. All I wanted was for them to stop screaming at each other.

"You little lying bastard," Mum hissed, her voice almost unnatural, warped and twisted. I shrank back, a moan in my throat. Pat suddenly cried out. I heard a wallop and a thump and I knew the sound. She'd thrown him against the wall again. Another violent crash was followed by the spluttering of static. The television was silenced.

I was frozen in the doorway, straining to hear something from Pat, so I knew he was okay. Then heavy footsteps stormed towards me across the rumpled carpet, so fierce I swore they shook the entire house. My nails dug into the door frame and chipped the paint away in thick flakes, and the cold and jagged fragments pushed their way underneath and shredded my skin.

Then the feet stumbled, and Mum screamed out just a few feet in front of me. Her wail was punctuated by a sickening thud. Now I heard the stuttering of footsteps across to my right, where the television had blared, then moving back again.

A second later, something nudged against my left boot. I dipped my head, only then realising that I'd gripped the door frame so tight that two of my fingernails had snapped clean in half, and hot trails of blood had seeped down to my knuckles. A flash of pain shocked my grip free.

"Pat?" I called, my own voice distant and barely recognisable, as I nursed my fingers. "Pat?"

"Oh, crap, crap, crap." That was him, to my right. "Joel, Mum's fallen over." He stepped further across the room, the squeak of his shoes terrifyingly loud. "She's tripped on the rug in those old slippers."

"Is…is she hurt?"

"I think she's hit her head on the edge of the cabinet." He stopped a few feet away. "I was waiting for her to get up, but…" The floorboards creaked as he knelt. "Blood."

My feet were locked in place. I leaned against the door while trails of sweat fled down the skin of my back.

"Is she okay?" My voice was barely a whisper.

"She's…she's not breathing. Uh, no, wait, she twitched…" His shoes squeaked as he rose and stepped back. He bent down again, then a second later gave a throaty grunt. "God, no. Maybe I should try revival."

I chewed my lip while Pat did what he could. Already my mind had forced gruesome images on me. Mum sprawled out on the carpet as vile sprays of blood jetted out from a gaping chasm in her forehead, then soaked into the thick fibres, turning them sticky and hot. The thought of it made me shake.

Pat quit soon after with a choking cough. "There's no pulse," he gasped. It sounded as if he was spitting up.

"No…no, there has to be. She only fell over. She can't be dead, Pat." After all, I'd fallen over and bashed myself good in the kitchen, but apart from a creeping headache, it wasn't anything serious. "She must be just knocked out."

"There ain't no pulse, I'm telling you."

"Are you sure you're doing it right?"

"I'm sticking my bloody fingers right in her neck, Joel. I can't feel crap. She's dead." Another pause, then a manic chuckle that was half-sob. "The wicked witch is actually dead."

I kicked away whatever had rolled against my boot, then crept forwards until my fingers found Pat. I crouched by his side. Reaching out, I brushed the softness of mum's cardigan sleeve then followed it up to her shoulder. She was lying on her back, her head twisted to the side and facing me. I pulled away with a whimper, then gently lowered my trembling hand to her face. My fingers traced across the warmth of her cheek to her mouth, then hovered over her lips, which were slightly parted.

When there was still no breath after a handful of seconds, I lowered my hand to her face and rested it there. Her lips weren't turned into a smile or a frown. They were just flat. Her eyes were open but her eyelids didn't flicker, not even when I shifted my hand and my palm brushed against them. Her eyelashes tickled my skin. It was like touching a mannequin, only her skin was still warm and soft.

Pat was breathing in an unsteady, frantic way.

"Maybe we should try again?" I whispered.

"No, no...the hell with it, she ain't coming back." He groaned. "Even if she did wake up, she'd just kill us instead, then go right back to drinking her bloody wine and watching her shows." He was silent for a second, breathing heavily. "I reckon we take this as an act of God."

I nodded, though I knew only too well that Pat didn't believe in God.

"How…How did she fall?"

"She tripped on the rug. She'd scuffed it up, and she's got those broken slippers, and she was trying to kick a wine bottle out of the way and she lost her balance. I suppose the bloody bottle killed her."

He left it at that, and although I didn't say anything, I knew he was right. The booze had finished her off, not by reducing her liver to ash as we'd often predicted, but by a much more simple and sudden approach.

We sat together in silence for what seemed like ages, right there next to Mum's body. I was still trying to work out what I should be feeling. Horror? Sadness? Relief?

In the end, I figured sadness would be most appropriate.

"What are we going to do now?" I asked, my palm still pressed to her face. "Should we call an ambulance?"

"I dunno. This place is a mess. She pushed me round the room right before she tripped over and did herself in. It looks like we had a fight in here. If the cops turn up, they'll probably think we killed her or summat."

"But we can just explain what happened."

"It's pretty much my word, though, ain't it? Even if they do believe us, you think they'll just let us live here by ourselves? Problem is, they'll find out I'm working under-age, and we'll be split up and sent off to some childcare agency or summat. You might end up in some weird institution place." Pat put his hand on my arm. "I'm not gonna let that happen."

"But what else can we do? We can't just leave her here." I swallowed. "She'll start to…you know, smell." Silence, and I could almost follow the tumbling, crashing path down the mountain of Pat's thoughts. "Pat, you don't want to bury her out in the garden or put her in the shed or something, do you?"

"Sod it." He shrugged and sat back. "We should just get the hell outta here. They'll catch us if we stay. Even if I could prove you were her bloody meal ticket, with your allowances she spent on herself, and I just let her get away with it all so we didn't get packed off somewhere – it won't make any difference…We've had it, if we don't leave."

"Where are we going to go, though?"

"I don't know." He looked around. "Maybe…maybe we could go and live with Uncle Bill for a while. He didn't seem to care how long we hung about last time we were there. Silly old bugger hardly even noticed us. I bet he wouldn't even ask how Mum's doing. There's no one else about for miles, we can just lay low."

"Okay, I guess."

I didn't feel like coming up with another plan, and didn't want to dwell on the fact that running away would just make us look even more guilty.

Truth is, I just wanted to get away, too – far, far away from this place. Even if we did end up in some desolate stretch of highlands with nothing but a crazy old man and a temperamental bird for company. Just the thought of being separated from Pat and stuck in some terrible orphanage turned my entire body numb.

And so we set about raiding the house. We grabbed anything that could possibly be useful – and a few things that couldn't, but which we refused to leave behind.

My Power Rangers alarm clock with authentic voice commands was a little bulky, not to mention childish, but it was the first present Pat had ever bought me with his own wages. I stuffed it in my tattered old duffel bag, along with enough clothes to last me a week. Hopefully we'd be at Uncle Bill's before seven days were up, else I'd have to start turning my underwear inside-out.

"Got everything you want?" Pat called into my room, and I nodded back. "Cool. I'm just gonna tidy up in Mum's room, then I'm gonna search it."

"Search it?" I began to stand up.

"Stay here," Pat said. "Won't take a minute. You know how she hides things, I bet she's got some loot stashed away behind all her old books. I've only got a hundred and change left from my last pay."

"What are you going to do about your job?"

"Ahh, hell with it. Won't miss me if I just don't show up."

He headed back down the corridor. A blare sounded as he tested the TV, then a series of vigorous tidying noises began to ring out from Mum's room, with the occasional grunt or frantic curse. I sat on my bed and waited, swinging my legs.

"Joel!" Pat's voice was shrill. "Come here, quick!"

"What is it?"

I sprang from the bed and shuffled into Mum's room. The side of my foot brushed against something soft just inside the doorway, perhaps a cardigan that Pat had discarded during his search. I knew that Mum was lying just a couple of feet to my left, and I edged away from that part of the room.

"I found summat. A box."

"What's in it?"

"There's a ton of postcards and some old pictures, junk like that. All the pictures, they're all of Mum and a random guy, and in some of them they've got a kid. I think the baby's me, and the guy's our Dad."

"Dad? Are you sure?"

"No, not sure, but...who else could it be?"

"What does he look like?"

"He's pretty tall, got a load of stubble. Looks like he's broken his nose a couple of times, too." Pat laughed. "I think you got his looks, man. Big eyes, and he's probably got dimples an' all – "

"But what's in the postcards? Did you read any yet?"

"Nah, that's why I called you in."

Paper rustled, then Pat cleared his throat. "Dear Milla. I hope you and Pat are both doing well, and the baby too. Please, please write back this time, I'm going crazy thinking about you all. Every time I call you don't answer, and it's got me worried something bad has happened. If you need money, I can send some. I just started getting back into work, it's only small stuff but it pays more than I need, so just let me know, okay? All my love, Darrel."

Pat sighed, and threw the letter on the floor. "Looks like we got stuck with the wrong parent, eh? Darrel sounds halfway normal. And generous."

"Why did she never mention him? Or show us his photo? She told me that she'd thrown them all out when I asked her."

I felt a bitter ball of rage churn in my stomach, and it almost came as a relief, as it was the first real thing I had felt since *it* had happened. That woman had robbed us of our father.

For my entire life I had wondered whether he'd left us, or if Mum had left him. I always wondered if he ever thought about us, or if he'd simply forgotten his past and moved on to a new life, a fresh start without us. This letter showed me at last, proved that he'd been forced away from us and shut out for good.

He was out there somewhere, and somehow I knew that even now he missed us.

"She's nuts, Joel. Was nuts. Whatever." He leafed through the postcards and whatever else lay in the box. "Looks like the same pub in every postcard. Place called 'The Prince Regent'."

"Where is it?"

"How the hell should I know?"

"Check the postmark on one of them."

"Oh, right. Looks like it says...Brookfields. The next bit's faded, but I think it says...yeah, I think it says London!"

"He lives in London?"

"Joel..." He paused for a moment, but I knew exactly what he was thinking from the way his breath had morphed into excited little gasps. "Maybe we should go there. To find him."

"I don't know," I said. I crushed my hands together. "London's huge. How are we going to track him down?"

"We already know the area he lives in. I'll search through these postcards, see if I can find an address for him."

I nodded hesitantly.

"Come on, even if we don't find him, it's gotta be better than living with Uncle bloody Bill on some sodding cliff top."

I pondered the idea of travelling the length of the country to find our father, a man we didn't even know.

To be honest, the thought of going to London scared me. From books and newspapers and films, the place seemed like a squalid, polluted dump where you got beaten up just for coughing in someone's vague direction. And then, while you were laid out in a bleeding mess on the floor, people would probably step right over you and continue with their day. Or maybe they'd film you writhing around on their phone and post it on YouTube.

"Well?" Pat gasped.

"Do you think we'll be safe there, in London?"

"Course we will, man. They're all wussy southerners down there."

"I guess." I swallowed back the crusty bile that had lodged in my throat. "It'd be good to meet Dad, huh?"

"Hell, yeah. He owes me fourteen years worth of Christmas and birthday presents." Pat laughed and punched me on the arm, a little too hard. "Okay, I'll set my alarm for 8.30am, we can head straight out to town and catch the first train to Dewsbury. Should be able to get to London from there."

Pat spent the rest of the evening flicking through the postcards that Dad had sent. Occasionally he came into my room to read out some.

In the end, it took Pat just under two hours to read them all, and he discovered surprisingly little.

Dad had left for London shortly before I was born, with practically nothing but a few notes and the clothes he was wearing. He found work with a man who he met in a bar (perhaps the Prince Regent?), although the details on that were sketchy at best. That was pretty much it.

After the final postcard Dad had sent, dated eleven years ago, we still hadn't found an address. He'd apparently given Mum his details, but she must have got rid of them, despite keeping all the postcards.

All we had to go on was the postmark that read Brookfields – which we found was just south of the Thames, thanks to the internet – and of course the pub in the pictures. According to a beer site, there was just a single Prince Regent in Brookfields. Pat scribbled the street name on the back of one of the postcards and slipped it into his bag.

Not much else seemed to be hidden in Mum's room, except for the odd half-empty bottle of booze. I didn't think we had enough info to find Dad, especially given the length of time since he'd sent those letters, but Pat had his mind set on our mission, and steeled himself like a soldier preparing for battle.

I set about investigating Brookfields on the internet. Research was slow because I had to rely on my text-to-voice software, which relayed website text through my speakers in an incredibly dull male voice with a grating American accent. I can't stand it, but Pat thinks it's hilarious because he can write swear words in my word processor and make the voice read it out loud. He used to do it all the time until Mum overheard it one day as she passed my room. She burst in and beat him around the head with her hairbrush, while the computer shouted out things like 'jizz monkey' and 'nob jockey'.

Eventually I found some kind of forum, where residents of Brookfields aired their thoughts on the area. I noted with some dismay that most of the users had recently had their houses broken into or their cars vandalised. It almost sounded like a competition for the most complaints. One woman lamented that her husband had been beaten up by the local vicar after complaining about the shortness of the Sunday service, but that didn't sound convincing, somehow. After ten minutes browsing the forum, I turned the computer off and sat rooted in my chair, gripping the armrests and silently rocking back and forth.

We were finally packed and ready for the trip by 11.30pm. Anxiety had set in, along with excitement and terror, and it was a worse mixture than coffee and sherbet. I was so wide awake I could have run a marathon, then turned right around and run it again. Pat insisted I head to bed anyway, and try to get some sleep so I wasn't grouchy for the morning.

"Oh, wait." I stopped at the door. "What about Chops?"

"Chops?" Pat asked.

"What if he comes back after we leave?"

"I dunno. We can't just leave the front door open for him or anything, someone might come in and find Mum."

"We'll have to leave some food out for him, though. He's not exactly a hunting dog, despite the way he goes on."

"Okay. We'll leave some tuna for him when we head out."

"And what are we going to do about Mum?" My voice dipped to a whisper, as if she could somehow hear us plotting.

"Whaddaya mean? She won't need food while we're gone."

"I mean, we can't just leave her like that, all sprawled out on the floor."

"Why not?"

"It's just not right. She's our mother, after all."

"Well, what do you wanna do?"

"I don't know." I sucked the tip of my thumb. "We should maybe put her back in her chair and cover her up."

"You want to lift her up? Maybe you should come over here and feel how big her stomach is first. She's pretty bloody huge after all those years…just sitting and watching TV."

"Can we at least cover her, then?"

"Yeah, okay, I guess. I'll grab a blanket." He pulled a rug from the hall cupboard and a warm gust of air caressed my cheek as he threw it over her body. "There ya go, she's all tucked in. Ha, she even looks kind of cute with all the pigs and donkeys on her."

"Oh no, you didn't use your old Winnie the Pooh blanket?"

"Yeah, so? Not like I need it any more."

"Yeah, but…"

"C'mon, bed for you." He ran a hand through my hair. "I'll wake you in the morning."

I lay awake for hours and listened to the distant ticking of the Swiss clock. My fingers were clenched around the corner of my pillow, hot and crumpled and slightly damp. I had the edges of the duvet tucked tight under my body, to cocoon myself in. Every so often I pressed the button on my watch to hear what time it was, to try and guess it to the nearest minute.

"Four sixteen ayy em," said Robot Judi on the 20th turn.

I sighed, then wriggled to turn over without disturbing the duvet shield. In the middle of the night, Judi's voice was even more creepy than normal. Still, I guess it was less creepy than the dead body lying right here in our house, just down the corridor from my room. But then...what if she wasn't really dead? Or what if she somehow came back to life, like her spirit managed to force its way back inside her body? Any moment now, she'd wake up and crawl out from under Winnie the Pooh's beaming face, gargling and retching up yellow bile. Then she'd stagger down the corridor and into my room, and tear back the duvet, and wrap her clammy hands tight around my neck...

I felt I had to check, just to be sure she was still there, and that she definitely wasn't breathing.

But I was far too terrified to leave the duvet shield and make my way into her room, and even more terrified to wake Pat up and ask him to check. He'd probably be even more grumpy and scary than a zombie Mum.

So I lay there too afraid to sleep, too afraid to get up, just playing my game with Robot Judi until it was finally morning and the jingly chords of Pat's alarm drifted from his room.

Part Two... Southward Bound

Four

It turned out that Mum really *was* dead, and hadn't moved from that spot all night. Pat laughed when I told him I'd been lying awake, too concerned to sleep in case our mother rose from the grave (or, in this case, from Winnie the Pooh) and massacred me before devouring my corpse. He said I was a big wuss with too much imagination.

My head was still throbbing, even worse than it had been after my fall, and Pat took me into the bathroom and unwrapped my bandages to take a look. He made that sound I really hate – the one where people suck in air through their teeth, which usually signifies that something is really very bad indeed but it's none of your business.

"What's wrong? Does it look infected?" I could practically feel my brains oozing from my skull. Had my skin turned black, and begun to wither and peel from my face?

"Nah, it's just a bit minging is all. Here, I'll clean you up."

He splashed some more Dettol on the cut, this time with no warning at all. The pain was worse than any noogie he had ever given me, and I almost bounced off the ceiling. I swear he did it on purpose, although he kept shouting, "Sorry!" between fits of laughter.

After I calmed down and stopped trying to beat him with my fists, he wrapped some fresh bandages around my head. At first he tied them too tight, and it felt like the oxygen was being squeezed from my brain, but luckily he loosened them just before I passed out. I felt kind of dorky with the thick strips pushing up my hair at bizarre angles, but I didn't really have much choice – it was either that or bleed out everywhere.

By now it was almost 8am, so we hurriedly filled every last space in our bags with food. By the end of it, I had the following stuffed in my bulging duffel bag:

Inventory for trip to London

7 x Boxer shorts
7 x Pairs of socks
7 x T-shirts
1 x Power Rangers alarm clock (with authentic voice commands)
1 x 'Rocktastic!' double CD (free with Sunday Mirror two years ago; present for Dad when we find him)
6 x Biscuits (chocolate)
10 x Biscuits (chocolate chip)
1 x Tub of sliced ham
1 x Jar of peanut butter

Finally, I took our Christmas Tree from the square plant pot on my windowsill and strapped it to the side of my bag, taking great care not to damage it. It wasn't a real tree, of course – just part of one. A spindly branch, to be exact. Mum would never have allowed us an actual full-size tree, and we were too poor to afford one anyway, so Pat had brought in the branch from our garden and stuck it in the plant pot, which I'd previously used to grow a potato for biology studies. I'd hung a folded-up Curly Wurly wrapper around the branch as tinsel, and Pat had sellotaped tic-tacs to the protruding twigs, like miniature baubles. We still needed a star for the top, and Pat had seen some of those small sticky ones that teachers used sometimes, but you could only buy them in bags of 500, which seemed a little wasteful. Still, the tree was fine as it was, and we always got it out from my closet on the first of December and replaced it on my windowsill. There was no way I was leaving it behind.

Heaving the handles of the bag over my shoulders, I staggered out of the door after Pat and waited for him to lock up. While I waited, I quickly made sure that the bowl of tuna for Chops still sat untouched at the side of the path. Then we hurried to the station, heading past the park and on up the hill to the centre of town. I listened out for any vaguely dog-like sounds as we strode by the edge of the forest, any barking or whimpering or even just the sound of something moving around in there. But aside from the rustle of leaves being swept up by the growing winds, the place was silent.

Eventually we reached the top of the embankment and I felt the first warming touch of the sun, although it was more of a swift prod than a lingering caress. The warmth disappeared and all that remained was the cold chill of the breeze that swept down the narrow 'high street' – which was not much more than a bumpy road containing a post office and a newsagents. From here to the station was only a short stagger, but the bag on my back was already aching my shoulders. I immediately regretted bringing along the Power Rangers alarm clock.

The first train to Dewsbury was already sat on the platform when we arrived, so we quickly bought our tickets and jumped aboard. Pat guided me to a table seat and we collapsed there, then dumped our bags by our feet and stretched out as best we could in the cramped space. The carriage smelled old, kind of musty and golden – that strange, inexplicable smell that all old things have, even old people. Not that I have some sick habit of sniffing pensioners, it's just something you notice when you're stuck in a post office full of them.

"Here we go then," Pat said, and he rubbed his hands together. "On our way to London. If we catch the 11.15 outta Dewsbury, we should be there for 5-ish."

"What are we going to do when we get there?"

"I dunno. Maybe head straight for Brookfields, see if we can find a hotel for the night, then start looking for Dad in the morning."

"Sounds good." I uncricked my neck and sighed. "I wonder how long it'll be before someone finds Mum." My mind was all over the place. Try as I might, I couldn't stifle the thought of her laid out back in our house.

"Hey, don't be so depressed, will ya? We're on holiday!"

"I'm just thinking, maybe we shouldn't have just left her there. Maybe we should call the police so they can go get her body or something."

"What, you nuts? You think they'll just say 'thanks for the info', and send someone round in a van to pick her up? They'll come looking for us, man. Think about it, how far we gonna get? Two brothers travelling alone, one of us blind an' all. It ain't exactly gonna take Crimestoppers to track us down, is it? We should wait till we find Dad, he'll come up with a plan."

The carriage door creaked open about thirty feet behind me, then a single set of footsteps echoed down the aisle towards us. They stopped halfway between the door and our table, and the newcomer struggled their way into a seat.

"Don't worry about it," Pat said, patting my hand. "Get some kip if you want, I'll wake you when we get there."

Even though I was exhausted, the jolting and grinding of the train kept me awake the whole journey. We eventually arrived at Dewsbury half an hour before the train to London was due, and our first stop was the ticket machine.

"Okay, lessee," Pat said. "Wow, they've stuck in one of those posh touch-screen machines. Looks like some prick's gobbed all over the screen, though. You got a tissue?"

I delved into my jacket pocket and handed him my single tissue. He stuffed it back in my hand a few seconds later. I clutched the soggy mess between two fingers and grimaced.

"Ugh, don't give it back!"

I threw it at him and wiped my palm across the front of my jacket.

"Quiet, ya big wuss, I'm trying to concentrate. Destination, uhh…London. Child's ticket I reckon." There was a pause of about two seconds, then a sharp intake of breath and the violent crash of fist meeting glass. "Forty-two frigging pounds for a frigging ticket! Just for one frigging train journey! Go frig yerself!"

You might have noticed by now that people have been saying 'frig' and 'crap' an awful lot, much more than they usually do in real life. This is because I've taken great care to censor any really bad words that crop up, which is unfortunately quite a regular occurrence, and I'm truly sorry for that. I don't mind swearing myself, mostly due to my gradual desensitising at the hands (or rather, at the mouth) of Pat. Still, I'd rather not type bad words out here in case any small children or overly sensitive people end up reading this, for whatever bizarre reason. The F-word does appear quite a few times throughout, but to be fair to Pat, he doesn't usually say that word much, mostly because Mum would always beat him about for it. Sometimes it just slips out if he's particularly angry. Or excited. Or surprised. Or tired.

He continued to rant at the ticket machine until I noticed the sound of heavy footsteps approaching. I tapped him on the arm and hissed at him to calm down. Unfortunately, I was a little too late.

"Can I help you, sonny?" The voice was deep and gruff, an elderly man, and his intonation suggested that he didn't actually want to help at all. He just wanted me and Pat out of the station and as far from him as possible.

"Oh, hey. I'm just taking my blind brother here to London, to see our Dad."

I sighed to myself, shaking my head. He was always using my 'condition' (another word I hated) to get sympathy, and although most of the time it worked, it was still incredibly annoying.

"But your tickets are well expensive," Pat continued. "Haven't you got owt cheaper than forty two quid?"

"Not unless you wait until after 8pm this evening to travel."

"8pm? Well, how much'll it cost then?"

"Okay, an evening saver ticket will be..." There was a series of light taps, like a pen being drummed against the edge of a desk. "Thirty eight pounds and fifty pence. Each."

"You kidding me? It's hardlies worth it."

"Sorry, those are the fares. I don't make 'em. Now, do you want tickets?"

"Don't have much choice, do we? Unless we sit on the bloody roof." Another pause. "Can we sit on the roof?"

"Are you serious? Do you want a ticket or not?"

"All right, fine." Pat slipped his wallet from his jacket pocket and money reluctantly exchanged hands. I heard the whirring of some kind of printer, followed by a brisk tearing sound.

"Have a good journey," the elderly man said.

"I hope we get a private cabin and a free massage," Pat replied, and the elderly man laughed.

"I think you're going to be disappointed, lad. Platform two for the next departure."

We still had 25 minutes to kill, so we found a bench and devoured our lunch, which consisted of slices of ham followed by biscuits. By the time the train rolled into the platform we had eaten over half of the ham and almost all of the biscuits, but I was still ravenous.

"I could really go for a pizza right now," I said.

I clutched my stomach and dreamed of our standard Saturday dinner, which we were set to miss out on. The savoury aroma of melted cheese and chunky pieces of spicy beef that filled the kitchen for hours after we'd finished eating.

We'd had pizza every Saturday for as long as I could remember, apart from one week when we decided to try an Indian takeaway instead. Pat ordered one of the hottest curries on the menu and had claimed it was too mild for his liking, but I knew he was lying because he struggled to even talk between mouthfuls. That, and he spent almost two hours in the bathroom the following morning. At one point I'd passed the door and was sure I heard him crying inside.

Just the thought of all that food was enough to cause a jet of stomach acid to geyser into my throat.

I swallowed it back and squeezed my arms around my torso.

"Don't even mention food," Pat said. "We've only got thirty quid now to do us till we meet up with Dad. Hopefully the guy's loaded, and he'll buy us pizza every night for the rest of our lives."

When the London-bound train pulled onto our platform, we claimed a pair of seats at the very end of the nearest carriage. The air in this train was even more stale than the last, as if the carriage was some long-lost tomb that had finally been cracked open after centuries of neglect. Even more disheartening was my seat, which contained less cushioning than an ironing board, but I settled in and squirmed until I was vaguely comfortable. I sat my bag on my lap, then pulled it open and fished around for the jar of peanut butter, which was tangled up in a pair of my boxer shorts.

"You gonna eat that by itself?" Pat asked. The disgust in his voice was obvious.

"Why not? Peanut butter is the best." I twisted the lid off and stuck my finger inside, then scooped a generous clump from the edge and raised it to my lips. My tongue smeared the sticky substance across the roof of my mouth.

Immediately I gagged, shocked at the bitter, repellent taste. My tongue shot out and my fingers clawed at the surface, to scrape away the disgusting gunk that had already formed into a crust. Pat burst into fits of hysterical laughter at my side.

"Hah hah hah! That wasn't peanut butter, man, it was marmite!"

"Bleghh, ughh, why thithn't you thell me, then?" I swallowed back the final remnants, then bashed my forehead against the seat in front to take my mind from the taste. "Urgghh, you, you switched the jars around in the cupboard!"

"No, I didn't. You must've just grabbed the wrong one."

"It's so vile. You really can't be human, eating that stuff."

"I'm surprised you didn't smell it when ya took the lid off."

"I wasn't paying any attention. Do we have anything to drink?"

"Nah, we only packed food. You should've asked before we got on the train, we could've got a can at that food stall."

"I didn't know I'd be eating marmite back then!"

"All right, calm down. The trolley guy'll probably come along in a bit." He stifled his laughter as best he could, but the occasional snigger forced its way out his nose. I felt like scooping out a handful of the marmite and pushing it right into his face, but he was the crazy fool that liked it in the first place, so he might even enjoy it.

The train finally pulled away just as Pat's laughter died down. I settled back, swilling spit around my mouth and forcing it down my throat to try and remove the stale taste. The carriage was well occupied and the hum of murmured conversation had grown pretty loud, an assortment of comments about the weather being 'dull and dreary'.

A man complained loudly that his seat was sticky, while two little kids argued over who could get the best score in Sonic on their DS. Someone close by had their MP3 player turned up far too loud. The chorus of Rick Astley's 'Together Forever' drifted through the chatter, or at least a tinny and distorted version of it. Rick sounded like he was only six inches tall and trapped inside a milk bottle.

As a quick side note, there's a good reason why I know who Rick Astley is – Mum owned one of his CDs (possibly his only CD), and when Pat was around ten years old, he used to sneak it up to his bedroom and play it all the way through. He never just *listened* to it, though. I could clearly hear him jumping around in there too, in some kind of heavy-footed, amateur dance routine.

One time I crept up to his door and listened while he had the CD on. I realised then that he knew all the words, because he was actually singing along. Not only did he know every word of every song, he sometimes even made up some new words to go in the bits where there was only music, and actually congratulated Rick for another fine performance at the end. It had taken all my willpower not to burst in and point and laugh. Instead, I stashed that memory away, ready to throw it back at him at some future point, whenever it was most needed.

"What a bloody racket," a middle-aged lady in front of me moaned. A man who must have been her husband grumbled in agreement, but it was obvious his attention was held by something that wasn't his wife.

"Youths of today, eh," Pat said. He elbowed me in the ribs. I elbowed him back, then turned and rested my head against the window, using my jacket as a pillow. Exhaustion won out, and almost immediately I felt my eyelids squeeze shut. The voices and hushed laughter and tinny music all blended into a single distant drone, then sunk without much of a fight into some subconscious part of my brain.

Until something amongst all that noise suddenly exploded to the surface.

I jerked my head from the window and my hand shot out to the side. I only meant to grab Pat's arm, but I flung out too enthusiastically. My knuckles caught him right in the jaw.

"Hey, what the hell? Why'd you thump me?"

"That sound!" I hissed, but it had stopped.

Pat tore my hand from his jacket. "What sound? What you talking about?"

"It's him!" I'd only caught it for a second or two, but there was no doubt. The ringtone I'd heard from somewhere inside our carriage was Mozart's Symphony Number 25.

Five

"He's on the train?" Pat whispered, his mouth just inches from my ear. A thick globule of spit landed on my temple. "How d'you know?"

"I heard his phone go off, just now! Quick, look about, see if anyone's on their mobile!" I waited, my fingernails dug deep into the fabric of the seat in front. Cold beads of sweat trickled down my forehead, and my stomach lurched with every jolt of the train. If the stranger from the park was here, he had to be following me.

"I can't really see, the seats are too tall. Oh, wait, crap. There's one dude down at the far end, sitting by the aisle. He's about fifty or sixty by the looks of it."

"Is he fat?"

"Nah, he's well skinny. Got shades on. Looks a bit like Ozzy Osbourne."

"It's not him, then, this guy was huge! Is there anyone else on a phone?"

"I don't know, man. How do you even know it's the guy? Probably just someone with the same ringtone."

"It was Mozart's Symphony Number 25. How many people do you know with that on their phone?"

"Um, I dunno. How does it go?"

"I can't really sing it for you!"

"Just hum it a bit, then. If it goes off again, I'll know what I'm looking out for."

I pulled his head close to mine and hummed the first few

bars, just loud enough for him to hear but no one else. The ringtone had come from somewhere in the middle of the carriage, at least five or six seats in front as far as I could tell, but I didn't want to take any chances.

"Doesn't sound familiar," Pat whispered when I was finished.

"No, I don't think it's been on any car adverts or anything."

"Crap. You really think this guy's following us?" I felt Pat crane himself up in his seat, to get a better view of the rest of the carriage.

"Don't be too obvious! In case he's watching us!"

"So what we gonna do then?"

"I don't know, I'm trying to think. I guess we have to work out what he looks like, so you can watch for him when we get off the train and tell if he really is following us."

"How we gonna do that? I can't just go and nick everyone's phone till I find the right one."

"Wait, wait…his aftershave!"

"His aftershave?"

"He had on some really nasty aftershave yesterday when he grabbed me in the park. Maybe he's still wearing it."

"Hey, hang on a sec. Your plan is to go 'round the train sniffing people?"

"Maybe if we just walk down the aisle together, I'll see if I can smell it. If I do, I'll cough into my fist. That'll be the sign that he's nearby. Then you just glance around and see if you can see a fat guy, and remember what he looks like, but don't be too suspicious when you're looking, okay?"

"Yeah, right. I really don't think this is gonna work. The guy's gonna see you having a coughing fit and work out summat's up."

"Come on, Pat. We have to do this, it's important. Please." He remained silent. "We might have some kind of crazy stalker after us! We need to know what he looks like."

"This is nuts, man. Really nuts." He sighed and tapped his feet against the floor while I sat there and pouted. "Fine," he finally whispered. "Come on then, let's go. But if this guy catches us and slits our throats, I'm blaming you."

Pat rose and I slid out in front of him, careful to steady myself against the rocking of the train. Then we gently made our way down the carriage, Pat just behind with one hand on my shoulder. I caught bursts of conversation from both sides, mostly mundane chatter about the ridiculous price of a sandwich from the buffet cart, or last night's episode of EastEnders. The thought that the fat man may be somewhere amongst them petrified me, and I had to force my legs forward. Occasionally I turned my head and sniffed as discretely as I could manage. I hoped it would just look like I had a cold, which would also justify the upcoming coughing fit.

We had already passed four rows, and so far nothing. I shuffled forwards as slowly as I thought I could manage without arousing suspicion. Occasionally my foot clipped the side of a bag or some discarded litter, and I had to hop to regain my balance.

Five rows. Two young children bickered to my right. Their mother warned them to be quiet, or they'd be getting off at the next station and going straight back home.

Six rows. I picked up a scent, an unpleasant smell, and I turned towards the source. It was rich and powerful, but it definitely wasn't aftershave. It smelled more like bbq sauce that had been left out in the sun.

Seven rows. My stomach felt like it was being tossed

around, like someone had ripped it out of me and stuck it in a washing machine. I drew in a deep breath and let it settle. Still no aftershave.

Then, just before we passed the eighth row, Pat's grip on my shoulder tightened and his nails dug into my skin. I almost cried out, but I managed to bite my tongue and keep on going. I didn't want to attract any more unnecessary attention. His grip relented a little, but there was a great sense of urgency about the way he prodded me forwards, almost knocking me off balance.

After the thirteenth row, I heard an automatic door just in front of us slide away. We stepped through. When it closed again, the voices of the other passengers were silenced and we were alone in the space between our carriage and the next. I turned to Pat and grimaced.

"Ow, you almost crushed my shoulder back there!" I rubbed the spot his nails had sliced. "What's wrong with you?"

"I think I saw him." Pat's words were hushed, almost too hushed to hear over the roar of the train.

"You saw him? The fat man? How do you know?"

"He was staring right at us. He just stared at us when we passed, and he was bloody huge, like you said he was. And I've definitely seen him before."

"You've seen him before? Where?"

"It took me a moment, but I remembered. He was on the first train, the train to Dewsbury. He was the only other person in our carriage."

"Oh, crap." Okay, the word I used was a little stronger than 'crap', but the situation called for it. The stranger was following us for sure – or perhaps just me. As far as I knew, he could've been camped outside our house all night, lying in wait. After all, how else would he be here, on the same train as us? He'd probably followed Pat and me to the park yesterday evening too, when we were in search of Chops.

A flood of panicked thoughts and ideas swelled inside my brain, like some kind of destructive maelstrom of terror. I had to lean against Pat with my head clutched in my hands, in case my skull exploded and showered the train with gore. The final thought that flashed through my mind was a terrible one, and I instantly tried to drown it amongst its brethren.

This stranger, this fat man who was stalking us, may have killed Chops to get to me.

"So what the hell we gonna do?" Pat asked. I shook my head. Part of me wanted to push my way back into the carriage and confront the stranger. Why was he following us, and what the hell had he done to our dog? But every twisted thread of common sense screamed it was a terrible idea. Pat's nerves had drained my own confidence, and I desperately tried to focus on our situation and come up with some kind of a plan.

"What we gonna do?" Pat repeated.

"I really don't know. Maybe just head back to our seats and pretend we're not on to him, then try and lose him when we get to London?"

"Man, I don't even want to go back in there. You should've seen him. He had tattoos down both of his arms, I couldn't even tell what they were, some kind of weird dragons or summat. And his arms were huge. I bet he could crush a car with his bare hands. Or rip a person's head right from their body."

"Okay, stop it already!"

"Oh, crap!" Pat suddenly hissed. He grabbed my arm and I almost jumped back against the door in surprise.

"What? What is it?"

"He's coming down the aisle towards us! I can see him through the glass door! Bloody hell, he's seen us! C'mon, move it!"

Pat pulled me away and I heard the opposite door slide open. Another burst of hushed conversation engulfed us. We rushed down the aisle and it took all my effort to keep up with Pat. I stumbled along behind him with his fingers wrapped tight around my wrist, while the train tossed us from side to side. My heart beat so hard it practically tore itself free, leaving my arteries dangling like damp socks.

We were maybe halfway down the carriage when the door behind us hissed open again, and I knew that it was the fat man. I could almost hear the strained gasps of breath and smell the body odour soaked into his shirt, just like when he grabbed me in the park. My skin began to itch and my bladder cramped. Suddenly I felt completely exposed, as if the stranger had a gun pointed at my back. People all around us were laughing and joking, but it was just background scenery, a host of disembodied voices that might as well have belonged to restless spirits. We were stranded in a long, desolate corridor – just me and Pat, and the fat man.

We reached the end of the carriage and fled through another door, and Pat rushed straight into the adjoining carriage, his hand still clamped around mine, cold and moist. I followed without a word, although a horrible realisation had dawned on me – at some point, probably soon, we would run out of train. What would the fat man do with us when he finally caught up? Would he kill us right here, on a train packed full of witnesses? Wrap his huge, muscular hands around each of our necks and pop them open like sachets of ketchup? I decided I really didn't want to find out.

"Are we nearly at the end of the train?" I panted. The door slid open behind us again.

"I think there's only a couple more carriages," he whispered back over his shoulder. He clearly had the same concern.

"What are we going to do when we reach the end?"

"I…there's a toilet sign at the end of the carriage," Pat said, and his voice rose into an excited squeak. "We can hide in there."

"But we'll be trapped!"

"Better that than being out here with that guy."

Another carriage door opened before us, and Pat came to a sudden halt. I was so intent on carrying on, so convinced that the fat man was just behind me, that I crashed right into Pat's back. He grunted, then swore under his breath. I heard a series of sharp knocks.

"Hey, anyone in there?" There was no reply. "Crap, the damn door's either locked or stuck." He pulled me away and we headed deeper into the train. More faceless voices drifted all around us, this time hushed – not a screaming kid or blaring iPod in the whole carriage. The place was so quiet, I was sure everyone would hear my heart throwing itself against my ribcage.

I staggered to my left as the train lurched, almost falling into the lap of a woman who shrieked with surprise right into my ear, before Pat jerked me back up and dragged me away. My face flushed, my cheeks red hot. The train lurched again a second later, but this time I stayed on my feet by grabbing hold of Pat's jacket. I realised then that the train wasn't just turning – it was also slowing down. A dull tone rang out through the carriage, then a deep, growly voice boomed out of overhead speakers, punctuated by bursts of heavy breathing.

"We are now approaching Willowsden. I repeat, the next stop will be Willowsden. Thanks for choosing to travel with UK Rail, please don't forget to take all baggage with you when you leave, and, uhhh, have a pleasant day." The message faded as we slipped through the doors.

"Carriage A," Pat said. "This is the last one." He squeezed my wrist and led me into the final box. The train had slowed to a crawl now, and I half-stumbled into a woman who was saying her goodbyes to a friend. As I was towed away, I mumbled a brief apology back over my shoulder.

"Is he still following us?" I asked Pat, wiping a sheet of sweat from my forehead with my sleeve.

"There's other people stood in his way, waiting to get off the train. We're screwed when they leave though, there's nowhere else to go."

"Why don't we jump off too?" It was a spontaneous thought that came from nowhere, probably a result of my hysterical fear, but all I could think about was getting off this train and as far from the fat man as possible. I thought Pat would tell me that leaving the train now was a stupid idea. I was wrong.

"Okay. Okay, let's do it!"

He pulled me to the very end of the carriage, and we stopped just short of the doors as the train jerked to a standstill.

"Where is he?" I whispered to Pat, my head twisted to the side.

"He's stuck at the other end. There's a dude with a huge suitcase blocking his way. He's still staring at us, man, it's really bloody creeping me out!"

"So he'll definitely see us get off?

"Yeah. You ready to run like hell when we get down on the platform?"

"Yeah, I think so." I wasn't sure if that was true at all. My legs trembled, and a deep itch ran under my shins that I was desperate to bend down and claw at.

"I'll keep a hold of you. Just keep up with me, okay?"

A moment later we pushed forwards and I felt a whip of cold air across my cheek.

"Step," Pat called out, and he dropped down in front of me.

I hopped straight out after him and landed feet-first on the platform, then we were off.

We broke to the left and charged alongside the train, the breeze full in our faces. Pat practically dragged me along behind him, going at such a pace that I could barely keep up. He suddenly twisted to the right, then cursed and yelled for someone to get out the way. We cut straight through a group of people and they shouted after us, but I didn't hear what they said. I didn't even care. I was too petrified, too desperate to keep up with Pat. I felt the fat man's hands closing in on me from behind, and knew that any moment now they would seize me and crush me until my spine burst.

The breeze suddenly cut out, and our footsteps were no longer the flat and hollow slap of soles on concrete, but instead boomed out all around us.

We were in some kind of tunnel. The air was damp and musty, and the overpowering stench of urine hit my nostrils and caused me to gag. I turned my head and spat. A trail of my own saliva streaked back across my cheek.

"Is he...behind us?" I managed to gasp. My voice echoed down the tunnel. Every breath I sucked in was amplified back, ten times as loud.

"I saw him come...off the train...but not sure if...he's following."

The echoes died as suddenly as they had appeared, and a ferocious gust of wind nearly took me off my feet. We had emerged at the other end. Now I could hear traffic just up ahead, cars screaming by at a terrific pace. We fought against the gales until finally we dragged ourselves to a standstill. I clutched my knees and concentrated on not being sick. I thought for a moment I would hurl for sure, but when I retched, nothing came up but hot air.

"This is ridiculous," I began to say, but Pat cut me off.

"Oh crap, he's still coming!" A fresh set of footsteps exploded down the tunnel towards us, cutting right through the howl of the wind. "He's like Michael pissing Myers!" Pat grabbed me and once again we were off, headed towards the traffic. My legs felt as if they were about to give way, just splinter and crumble beneath me and disappear with the gales. My throat had practically closed up, and every breath was a battle. But still we ran.

The roar of passing vehicles was intense now, and I could feel them raging before us. I pulled back against Pat's grip, too terrified to go any further.

"Where are we going? It sounds like we're heading towards a motorway!"

"That's cos we are!"

"What? Well, is there some sort of bridge?"

"No!"

That wasn't the reply I'd hoped for.

"Joel, you gotta trust me, okay? Stick with me, don't fall or anything." The fat man's footsteps were no longer booming forth from the tunnel. He was out, and closing in on us. I knew I didn't have a choice – or rather I did, but the option to stay here and fall into the stranger's grasp was even more unpleasant than what I realised we were about to do. Before I even had the chance to nod, Pat dragged me towards the traffic.

Six

Pat practically threw me over the waist-high wall that ran alongside the motorway. I landed on my arse on some kind of grass verge, but it may as well have been concrete because my spine almost shattered on impact. The traffic thundered past just a few feet away, the wail of their engines terrifyingly loud, their tyres trembling against the road. The entire ground vibrated beneath me. A car blasted its horn as it sped by us, and I collapsed back against the wall and pressed myself flat against the rough bricks.

"Come on, get up," Pat screamed over the noise. He grabbed my shoulders and heaved me back onto my feet. "He's right behind us!"

"I don't – "

I had no chance to continue. He snatched my hand and towed me along the edge of the road. A moment later, the gust from a passing truck threw me against the wall, and the roar of its wheels sliced right through my skull. My muscles instantly turned to stone. I clung to the bricks with my free hand and listened to the truck's horn fade into the distance.

"Hurry up," Pat screamed. He crushed my hand in his. "The fat bastard's coming over the bloody wall!"

"I can't do this," I yelled back. My knuckles were close to popping out of joint. "I can't!"

"There's a gap in the traffic after these next two cars! We've gotta get across, okay?

"Pat, I can't!" The first car hurtled past.

"There's a steep jump down onto the road, so be careful!"

As the second car flew by, Pat pushed away from the wall. I felt him drop and I leapt down after him, landing hard on the tarmac. Immediately Pat dashed towards the centre with me just a step behind. I could already hear more cars speeding towards us. They were horribly close - the howl of their horns merged into a terrible squealing sound. Tyres screeched in unison as the drivers slammed on their brakes. I cried out, my voice lost somewhere amongst the din. All I could think of was a truck slamming into us and tossing our mangled bodies high across the road, before our remains crashed back down to the tarmac and bounced along like gory blood sacks.

The next thing I remember, Pat's arms were around me. He dragged me to a halt and clutched me to his chest. The screeching tyres and blaring horns tore past us and disappeared down the motorway.

"Where are we," I asked, the side of my face crushed into his jacket. His buttons dug into my cheeks, but I was so relieved that I could feel anything at all.

"Central reservation. Crap, this was a bad idea."

"I told you that just a minute ago."

I twisted my head to the side. I could only just make out the broken strains of another voice over the roar of the traffic. A man, shouting from the other side of the road.

"Is that him?"

"Yeah. Can't hear a word of it, but he looks well pissed off. Come on, we gotta get to the other side before he makes it over."

We had just clambered over the barriers separating the two sides of the motorway when a siren kicked into life about a hundred yards to our left. Pat cursed and grabbed a hold of my jacket.

"Cops! Quick, they're slowing the traffic! Leg it!"

He sprinted forwards, almost yanking my arm clear from its socket and giving me whiplash in the process. The sirens grew louder until my eardrums felt as if they would shatter and explode right there in my head, but we made it to the far edge of the motorway and burst up another grass verge. At the top there was another wall and Pat once again shoved me clean over it. This time I landed on my hands and knees, but there was no grass and dirt to cushion my fall as there had before – this time, there was only jagged rock.

"Ahhh, ow!"

"Get up, Joel, the coppers are pulling over!" Once again I was yanked to my feet and once again we took off, choking and gasping and spitting all the way. After just a few feet the concrete ended. We sprinted on through soft mud, and I kicked up great chunks with every step. Something pointed brushed through my hair and I ducked out of its grasp.

"Are we in a forest, or something?"

"Yeah, kind of. Just keep going!"

We ran on for another minute or so, until our legs finally gave up beneath us and we collapsed in a heap. Then we nestled ourselves amongst the crisp leaves and cold, damp layers of moss. My chest heaved, desperate for air. I sucked in great lungfuls of the sedative scent of pine needles and dried wood.

My breathing took almost three whole minutes to return to normal, but even then my legs still ached and my palms were sore where the skin had been scraped back. The back of my head was cold and wet, half-buried in dirt, but I could have happily laid there for as long as I lived. Considering all the shocks my heart had taken, that probably wouldn't be very long anyway.

"Oh, man," Pat gasped beside me. He coughed up a hunk of phlegm, which he thankfully spat on his other side. "My clothes are all sweaty and dirty and minging, and my clean ones are in my bag on the bloody train."

"Same here." Not only had I lost all of my spare clothes, but also any remaining food – although the marmite wasn't a huge loss – as well as my Power Rangers alarm clock and the Christmas tree. So far, today had been pretty bloody lousy. "Do you still have the money?" I braced myself for the reply.

"What's left of it. Still got our tickets too. We'll have to grab another train down to London."

"What if that guy's waiting at the station for us to get back?" My question was answered with silence, for a few seconds at least.

"I wish I knew who that twat was," Pat muttered.

"Whoever he is, he doesn't seem to like us much. Do you think he knows what we did to Mum?"

"We didn't do owt to Mum, and how would he know anyway? Only way he'd have found out is if he broke into our house after we left."

"Yeah, and I guess he couldn't have done that if he was following us." I lay there and ran my hands through the leaves, occasionally grabbing a handful and feeling them crumble in my grasp. Then Pat said something that caused me to sit bolt upright, undoubtedly with a shocked expression plastered across my face.

"Joel, I...I think I might know who he is."

"What? You know him?"

"I don't know him, I just might know who he is. But I'm

not certain." He sighed again and kicked his feet through the undergrowth.

"Well, who do you think he is?" There was a moment of awkward silence before Pat finally answered.

"You know how I said I worked at a plastics factory?"

"Yeah."

"Well, that wasn't really true. It was a bit of a lie."

"What do you mean? Where do you work then?"

"It's kinda complicated." He sighed again, and I felt a deep sense of unease creep through my insides, like a stain spreading through a tablecloth. "You know Matty Phillips, guy I went to school with? Gruff voice and says 'innit' a lot?"

"Yeah, you brought him round a couple of times. What about him?"

"Well, me and him work for his older brother, doing odd jobs. All cash-in-hand stuff."

"Okaaaay," I said, nodding slowly. "What kind of jobs?"

"Well, that's where it's a bit tricky, see. Some of the stuff we do's slightly...illegal."

"Slightly illegal?" The unease turned to alarm. I dug my fingers into the soil at my sides and pulled up great clumps of mud and shrivelled weed roots. "What counts as slightly illegal?"

"Ya know, just things like transporting hooky goods. Not really breaking the law, just bending it a bit."

"I'm not sure that's slightly illegal," I said, resting my head on my knees. "Either something's illegal or it's not, and that sounds illegal."

"Oh come on, what are you, the angel on my shoulder? It's not like we're mugging old ladies. It's mostly just electrics, stuff that's come from factories and ain't gonna be missed."

"But what's this got to do with the fat man? Did you steal some stuff from him?"

"I don't know, that's the thing. I was wondering, maybe he's one of the guys me and Matty work for. We only ever deal with Matty's brother, I don't see anyone else who's involved."

"But why would they be following us? And why would the guy come after *me* in the park?"

"That's the other thing." He rustled through the leaves again, then I heard something hard bounce off a nearby tree trunk. My head jerked in its direction. "Sorry," Pat said, "that was just a rock."

"What's the other thing then?" I asked, knowing full well that I didn't want to hear the answer.

"Sometimes, when we're dropping off stuff for Matty's brother, I keep a bit back for myself. Like last week we had to deliver some sim cards, and I pocketed a box to sell on for some extra cash. I'm careful when I do it though, not even Matty knows about it."

"You steal the stuff that was already stolen?"

"It's only ever a tiny amount, not enough for them to notice even. Well, that's what I reckoned anyways."

"But you steal stolen goods from criminals?"

"I don't have a choice," he shouted back, and the change in his voice set my heart racing. "I'm the only one who supports us, me and you, Mum was bloody useless! But no one wants to hire some poxy fourteen-year-old. Not even that stinking old plastics factory. The best I could do would be shifting trolleys about at the bloody supermarket, for three quid an hour!" I shrank back against the twisted tree roots, my knees pulled up to my chest. I'd never heard him like this before. "Even with all the jobs I did for those guys, all the risks I took, it wasn't enough! Not with Mum spending all our frigging benefits on booze!"

I found myself nodding, but I was numb to his words. The shock and exhaustion that had built up since yesterday morning had left my mind a dripping mess. The seriousness of what Pat had just told me, the nature of his work – it was like it didn't really matter. As if he'd just confessed he was an avid stamp collector. I finally realised the lengths he was willing to go to just to keep us together. Our screwed-up, broken little family.

"I'm sorry, Pat." A weak grin spread across my lips, an involuntary reaction. "How come you never told me?"

"I dunno. I guess…ahh, forget it." Something bounced off my leg and settled amongst the leaves. "C'mon, get your arse out that mud. We should head back to the station."

I groaned but pulled myself to my feet, then we moped back in the direction of the motorway. The cars and trucks were no more than a distant rumble, and it was only then that I realised how far we had run before. At the time, I guess I had been concentrating on not passing out instead of where we were actually going.

"So you think the fat man is someone you've stolen from, and now he knows we're on the run, and he's coming after us?"

"Maybe. It's just a theory."

"But why would he be following us? Wouldn't he just kill us, like in the Godfather or something?"

"I haven't nicked owt from the mafia, Joel. Least I hope I haven't. And like I said, it wasn't like I stole anything big, it was just pieces here an' there, whenever I had the chance. Ugh, what the hell is going on?"

"Maybe you accidentally took something really valuable from them. Like an MP3 player with diamonds stashed inside.

Maybe they're tracking us cos they think we're going to sell the diamonds on, and when they catch us, they're going to take the diamonds back and bury us in concrete and dump us in the river." The thought made me shiver. "We'd be nothing more than a pile of bones encased in a slab of rock. Imagine that. No one would even know you were there." I wondered for one morbid second what Mum would think of us abandoning her body on her bedroom floor, her burial comprising of no more than a dirty old sheet featuring fictional talking bears.

"Whatever. We better be careful is all I know."

"Well, it's up to you to keep watch for the fat man."

"He ain't hard to spot, believe me. Besides, you can probably hear him a mile off. He's like Godzilla, the way he stomps about."

When we reached the motorway again, I hid behind a tree while Pat crept ahead and scouted for any policemen that were still around – or, of course, the fat man. Dried leaves and twigs crunched under his boots, marking every step. He stopped about thirty feet ahead. The only sound then was a light scratching far above me, the sound of tiny claws digging into bark.

A moment later Pat returned and crouched down beside me. The scratching disappeared.

"No sign of 'em," he said. He grabbed my arm and spat into the leaves. "C'mon, let's find a way across."

This time we didn't go for the direct approach, for the sake of keeping our bodies in one piece.

Instead, we walked along the side of the motorway until we came across an underpass, and Pat led us to the other side and back towards the station.

Walking back through the tunnel was the hardest part of the

return journey. The damp chill that hung in the air caused my skin to tingle, and the terrible smell of stale urine still lingered, somehow even stronger than before. Even though we crept forwards, our footsteps still sounded like miniature explosions amplified all around us. Pat's grip tightened on my arm, until he'd almost cut off all circulation.

"That's starting to hurt," I whispered, and he relaxed a little.

"Sorry."

"Still nothing?"

"No, can't see anyone. I bet the bastard's hiding at the other end though. Ready to jump out as soon as we step outside."

When we emerged at the other side again, we stopped for a moment and waited. I braced myself, fully expecting the earth tremors that signalled the fat man's approach. Thankfully, there was nothing except the distant sound of a mother screaming at her child to calm down. I should have been relieved, but somehow the peace was just as terrifying.

"Still nothing?" My words came out in a nervous stutter.

"You gonna ask me that every ten seconds? If you find you're being dragged along backwards, that means I've spotted him and I'm running away, okay?"

"I was just checking." I kicked him with the side of my foot.

"Hey, stop it, will ya! C'mon, there's no one about."

We continued on in silence, and I listened for any kind of disturbance or movement that might give the fat man away. With our brisk pace we arrived back at the train station in no time at all. Pat decided to head in and perform his usual reconnaissance duties, but first he propped me against a wall near the entrance.

"Are you sure this is a good idea?" I asked, my lip clenched in my teeth.

"Hey, no worries. I'll have a quick scan, make sure the coast's clear. There's people about so if anyone tries to grab you, just shout." He had a certain glee in his voice, and I began to wonder if he was actually enjoying himself – maybe he thought he was James Bond Junior or something.

"What if he covers my mouth, or holds a knife to my throat," I began to protest, but Pat had already skipped off.

As soon as his footsteps had faded from earshot, I shrank back against the wall. I tried to push myself into it and merge with the bricks. I felt exposed, just as I had back on the train, and couldn't shake the feeling that hundreds of eyes were burning into me. Pat's name was poised on my lips, but instead of calling out, I just dipped my head and listened to the sound of my own heaving chest. Each breath came just milliseconds after the last, like machine gun fire.

My concentration was suddenly broken by footsteps across to my left, and I realised they were headed straight towards me. My fingers clawed at the bricks behind, scraping the skin of my fingertips.

"Pat?" I called out. "Pat, is that you?"

No answer. Whoever it was they were close, maybe only twenty feet away, and I knew that to get away I would have to run right now – tear myself from the wall and fly back towards the tunnel. I knew the way, I knew I could do it. But then where would I go from there? How would I find Pat again? Hesitation and doubt kept me locked in place, and it was too late to escape now. Whoever it was, they were standing right beside me...

"Boo!"

"You arse," I hissed, and I punched Pat in his gut. He

grunted but kept on laughing – a long, dry chuckle that raised my anger levels to a single bar below 'kill for revenge'.

"Your face! What a sight, man!"

"You scared the crap out of me! I thought you were the fat man!"

"Nah, there's no sign of him. He must've legged it when the cops showed up. Maybe they even arrested him, if we're lucky. Come on bro, there's a train in ten minutes. Let's wait at the far end till it arrives."

"I hate you."

I continued to give Pat a hard time, and he continued to protest that I had no sense of humour. Maybe he was right. But after everything that had happened (was it really only yesterday that all this started?), I really hadn't felt like myself. My mind churned constantly, going over every tiny detail of the past twenty four hours, but the more I thought about it all, the emptier I felt inside. Were we really doing the right thing here? Was there even a right thing for us to do?

The train came on time, at exactly 'half past two pee em' according to Robot Judi. We didn't board straight away. Pat kept watch along the length of the platform first, in case the fat man suddenly reappeared and sneaked onto one of the other carriages. We waited there until the guard blew his whistle, then we climbed onto the end carriage and took a seat in the first row. A few passengers were already inside, occasionally announcing their presence by shuffling in their seats, coughing, sighing or blowing their nose.

"I keep waiting for you to tell me this is all a big joke," I whispered to Pat as the train pulled away. "Mum's not really dead, we don't have gangsters chasing us, and this is just a surprise trip down to London. We'll spend a couple of days there, then head back and everything will be just the same as before." I smiled and shook my head.

"Wish I could tell you all that," Pat eventually replied. "But we couldn't have lived like that much longer anyways. Even if…if the accident hadn't happened, we still would've left, eventually. I'd thought about it loads before. Couple of times I'd been close to waking you up during the night and sneaking off. Leave her behind. Probably could've walked out during the day, like, and I doubt she'd have noticed. Or cared. Bollocks to it anyway."

I rested my head against the window and let the vibrations tremble through my skull and down my spine. In minutes I was asleep. I dreamed that Dad took me and Pat to a sprawling fun fair, which smelled of sweat and salt and burned nuts. He bought us candy floss which tasted of mint liquorice, then we rode a rollercoaster which kept on going up and up and up. I asked Pat if we were near the top yet, but he didn't respond, except to burst into a scratchy rendition of 'Never Gonna Give You Up'.

I never had a chance to reach the peak, as a particularly violent tremble shook me awake and it took me a moment to regain my bearings. Pat was asleep at my side, his elongated snorts a mark that he'd been gone some time. I settled into his shoulder and smiled. When I next stepped off this train, we'd be there – we'd be in London.

Of course, if I'd known right then how our trip to London would turn out, I would've left the train at the very next stop and run all the way up to the barren highlands of Scotland, to live with Uncle Bill instead.

Seven

Despite the uncomfortable posture, I somehow managed to grab a few hours of broken sleep on the train. When I finally woke up, my neck was stuck solid in one position (to the left and back a little), and I had dribbled all the way down one cheek. I dabbed at the spit with the back of my hand and rolled my tongue around my sticky mouth. Again I wished we'd brought something to drink.

"So thirsty," I croaked.

I rolled my head in small circles and winced at the spasms of pain that shot down to my shoulder.

"We'll be there in about twenty minutes, the driver reckons." Pat stifled a yawn. "Man, I'm bored. You ain't much fun when you're asleep."

"What does it look like outside? Are there lots of huge buildings?"

"Nah, just some grotty-looking flats. I hope Dad doesn't live in a craphole like that."

We discussed what Dad would be like when we finally met him. Whether he would be pleased to see us, whether he would be fantastically rich, and whether he would have married another woman after leaving Mum.

"I just hope he didn't sign up with another psycho," Pat said with a sigh.

"He probably learned his lesson after Mum kicked him out. I don't think I'd ever want to go out with another woman in my life."

"You'd just be celibate?" Pat laughed again. "No way, man. I couldn't give up girls even if they were all nuts."

"How would you know? You've never even had a girlfriend."

"Shuddup, ya little nob. Like you've ever been out with a girl."

"I never get a chance to meet girls! I practically live in my room!"

"You used to," Pat corrected. "Anyway, sure there'll be plenty of fit southern ladies down here we can work our magic on, eh?"

"I don't really care, anyway. Girls always lead to trouble."

"What you babbling about?"

"In books and films and stuff. The girl always gets kidnapped, and then the good guy has to chase after the bad guys to rescue her."

"Yeah, that's true. Like in Super Mario Brothers, right? If I was Mario, I'd seal the Princess in concrete and wire the whole lot to explode if Bowser's ugly arse went anywhere near it. How many games have there been, eh? And it's always the same. Thick little moustache man never learns."

Our deep philosophical conversation was interrupted by a sudden crackling sound from just above, like radio static, followed by a resounding 'dink'. A startled murmur rose from the other passengers.

"Ah, crap," Pat said. He shuffled in his seat and placed his hand on my shoulder.

"What is it? What's going on?"

"It's the lights, they've all gone off. The whole carriage is dark. Great this is, eh? All that money to sit in the dark on some arse-numbing seat."

"At least we're almost there."

"Yeah, well, I guess so." He shifted again and I rested my head against his bony shoulder. A chill had crept through the carriage, so I hitched my knees up to my chest and propped my feet on the edge of my seat.

"Will you tell me more about the work you did?" My voice was hushed, so no one else overheard.

"What, the stuff for Matty's brother? There really ain't much to say. It's just simple jobs. Mostly just foot work, picking up merchandise and dropping it off."

"Oh," I said, and I frowned and squeezed my legs. I realised then I was a little disappointed by Pat's reply, as if I'd secretly hoped he was some kind of gangster who went about capping fools, or whatever it is that gangsters do all day. Of course, I didn't really want for that at all, but I'd at least hoped for something a little more intriguing or exciting. Pat must have picked up on my discontent, because he cleared his throat and leapt back in.

"It's still dangerous, though. There's this one time we almost got caught by the cops with a box of hooky posh watches. That was well scary."

"Really?" I turned towards him with a grin. "What happened?"

"Me and Matty, we'd just lifted these watches from the loading bay of Spencer's, that big, posh department store up in Lowerstofte. He kept watch while I grabbed it, then we legged it away down all these back streets and stuff, me carrying this big box full of Rolexes or whatever.

"Anyway, we come out on the high street, ready to jump on the bus, and we spot these two coppers walking along the pavement towards us. They're getting closer and closer, and they're both staring at us with these really stern expressions, like they know what we've done." His voice was hushed now, and I leaned in further. "And then the bus comes around the corner, just behind them, so it's coming towards us, and I'm praying for the bus to overtake the coppers and get to us first, right? But then some doddery old woman starts to cross the road and the bus has to stop and wait for her, so there's no way the bus is gonna get to us before the cops. And Matty's having a heart attack next to me. I mean, he's completely pale and he's swearing under his breath, and the box is getting heavier and heavier in my arms. I just wanted to drop it and run, just get out of there, ya know? And my hands were so sweaty, I knew I'd drop it soon anyways."

"So you ran from the cops?" I said, my mouth wide open.

"Nah, we didn't have to. They just walked right by us, thank God. We got on the bus and went home."

He paused for a moment, and I sat there in bewildered silence while the hideous anticlimax settled in my stomach like bad custard. I couldn't have been more disappointed if I'd gone to some posh ice cream parlour and ordered a triple-scoop toffee surprise with extra fudge sauce, and the waitress had brought me a plate of spam instead. And then spat on it.

"That story really sucks."

"Piss off, man, it was terrifying at the time! We could've been nicked! Might've been sent to some borstal or summat."

"Whatever."

"What's up with you, anyways? You were all appalled when I told ya what I did for cash, and now you're saying I'm boring?"

"Nothing's up with me." I wrapped my arms around myself again, then rested my chin on my knees. The seat seemed even more rigid than before, and my legs had turned almost completely numb. At that moment I thought of my duvet, and how warm and safe I always felt beneath it, all sheltered and hidden away from the world. I wished that I was back in my room and cocooned inside it, even with the risk of Mum coming back as a zombie.

Ten minutes later, the driver announced that we were pulling into the station. My stomach pulsed inside of me, a frantic bag of nerves and excitement, and we immediately pushed out of our seats and took up position beside the door. The train finally came to rest with a shudder that almost knocked me off my feet.

"Here we go then," Pat whispered. "We're officially southerners."

The first thing that hit me when I hopped down onto the platform was a tornado of noise that whipped all around us. There must have been rows and rows of trains lined up either side of ours. They growled like an army of wolves. People swarmed past us on both sides of the platform, their suitcases and offspring dragged right along behind them.

The next thing that hit me was the smell. I had never been to London before, or any big city really, so the aroma was something I'd never experienced in my entire life. Smoke, sweat, perfume and a hundred other scents that I couldn't even identify, all mixed together in the frosty air. I was overwhelmed by the concoction and sucked in great gasps until my chest hurt.

The final thing that hit me was a lady's suitcase as she pushed her way past.

Pat grabbed my wrist and led me down the platform, straight after the hordes. I clung onto him and tried desperately not to catch his heels as we pushed our way through the frenzied swarm. An elbow caught me just above my ear, an inch short of my wound. I tilted my head away to adjust my bandage. There was no apology, mumbled or otherwise, from the culprit. Someone else clipped my leg a second later and I found myself growing anxious, as if I was trapped in some mindless stampede. A sea of bodies with no real aim, other than to get as far away from this place as possible. The constant trundle of wheels and stomping of boots surrounded me. At that moment I felt more bewildered than ever before, tangled in a blanket of strangers.

We eventually made it to the end and swerved our way through the station, adding fresh bruises to our collection from the flailing limbs and bags of the crowds. I yelped as the edge of something hard slammed into my shin.

"Y'okay?" Pat called back. I barely heard him over the din of the crowd.

"Just about!"

We finally prised ourselves free of the station and staggered out into a heavenly cool breeze. It was like downing a glass of ice water after eating a whole party pack of ready salted crisps. Actually, that feeling came a moment later, when Pat spotted a drinks machine and bought us a can of cola. Of course, first he had to complain about the price.

"A quid fifty? For a bloody can? You've gotta be kidding me! Everyone down here must be millionaires, man!"

"Please, Pat, I'm so thirsty! I feel like I'm going to throw up. My legs are numb."

"All right, all right, calm down."

The second the can was slapped into my palm, I cracked it open and tipped it to my mouth. I guzzled the icy liquid so fast that thick, sticky trails spread across my cheeks, then ran down my neck and soaked my t-shirt. It felt so good. I didn't even taste the cola until I was finished, and the only reason I stopped was so I could take a breath and belch.

I held the can out for Pat, but he didn't take it. He was muttering something under his breath, something I couldn't quite make out. All I caught was the last few words.

"Hey, what the f…" He turned so fast that his shoulder caught my jaw. I stumbled back against the machine. The plastic cover trembled and pushed me away again. "Hey," Pat yelled, then I heard him take off, sprinting away from the station. Before I could shout after him, he called back: "Stay there, Joel!"

"Pat? Pat, what's going on?" The can slipped from my grasp and clattered along the ground. No response. His footsteps had vanished into the crowd, a buzzing wall of voices that completely enclosed me. I was alone.

I pressed myself against the machine and tried to stay calm. For a while it worked. I cleared my mind and concentrated on the cool plastic screen beneath my palms. Then someone stepped in front of me.

"Pat?" I croaked, but the footsteps were far too heavy.

"Come out the way, will ya?" The voice belonged to a woman, but only just – she sounded as grizzled as a heavyweight wrestler.

"S-sorry?"

"Out the way, kid, I want a drink!"

"Oh!" I slid to the side. The woman's coins rattled in the slot, then a can hit the tray with a *thunk*. She disappeared again.

When I checked my watch, Robot Judi said the time was 6.30pm. I waited in that spot and prayed for Pat to return. An endless stream of strangers pushed past me, and my heart leapt every time someone came up to the machine, just in case it was him. Usually I would get a blast of smoke in my face, or a bag in the shins. I bit my lip and edged as far out of the way as possible.

Every minute or so I checked the time again. By 6.50pm, huge salty tears burned my eyeballs. The sound of choking laughter cut through the din, and I just knew that it was aimed at me. They all stared at me as they passed, I could tell – stared and pointed and fell about at what a pathetic sight I was. The breeze was no longer refreshing. Instead, it was cold and unfriendly.

"You got some change, kid? For a cup of tea?"

The voice caught me by surprise. Someone – a man – was stood by my side. I never heard him approach, and at first I wasn't even sure if he was talking to me, or some other kid that just happened to be stood by the can machine.

"Hey, kid, you deaf? Hello?"

"Hello?" I ventured. The word came out as a squeak.

"Hey, he speaks! You got some change I can borrow?"

"Change? No, nothing." I ground my teeth together and repeated two words – GO AWAY – as loudly as possible in my head. If I did it over and over again, surely he had to psychically pick up on it.

"Come on, you must have something, kid. You here by yourself, eh?"

There was something sinister about the way he said that. The hairs on my neck pricked up, and a nervous ache crept through my stomach. Suddenly I wondered if he was working with the fat man. As soon as he was sure I was alone, he'd bundle me into the back of a van and that would be that. The next time anyone saw me, I'd be a sack of bones at the bottom of the Thames.

"No, I'm not alone! I'm here with my parents!" My face burned with the lie. I was sure the man would pick up on it, so I turned away.

"All I need is a pound. Come on, kid. Just a pound."

GO AWAY! GO AWAY! GO AWAY!

"I don't have rich parents like you," he said, and he stepped closer. I could feel his breath on the back of my neck.

"I'm sorry," I yelped, then I pushed away from the drinks machine and staggered out into the wall of noise. Terrifying voices swarmed around me, loud and unfamiliar and somehow warped, as if they belonged to demons. I forced myself on, one step at a time. I had no idea if the man followed, but I was certain I could still feel his breath on my neck.

"Watch it," a demon muttered as it brushed past me. I staggered to my side, then pushed on. My muscles were so tense that my entire body was stiff. My limbs felt like they were bound in splints. I held my arms out before me and stumbled through the chaos, desperate to find the exit from this netherworld.

Something hard caught my leg, and this time I was thrown to the ground. My palms were shredded against the rough concrete as I desperately tried to stop myself. My knee smashed so hard that I cried out. I rolled over onto my back, clutching at the mangled limb. Devils continued to stomp past on all sides. I was sure they would crush me and just keep on going, until there was nothing left of me but a puddle. I curled into a ball and squealed, braced for the end.

Eight ⠦

Two hands suddenly grabbed me just below my shoulders, and the next I knew I was being lifted and dragged away. I kicked and squirmed, but a woman's voice told me:

"Hey, it's okay! It's okay!"

I was back on my feet, but I couldn't put any weight on my injured knee or else it screamed in agony. The woman had a hold of my arm and she led me away. I hobbled as best I could. She was still talking, asking me questions, but my mind was all over the place. My heart thumped against my ribs, like it was desperate to break free of its bony prison.

"…your leg? Is it okay?"

"My knee hurts."

"Where's your family?"

"I…"

I wondered how to answer that. Definitely not with the truth – Mum's wrapped in a Winnie The Pooh blanket on the floor of her bedroom, my brother ran off and left me, and with any luck Dad will be in the pub I'm looking for.

"…I really don't know."

"You're lost? Right, let's go, come on."

Once more I hobbled after her. Again she asked me questions, and again I could barely concentrate on her voice. I wished with all my might for Pat to return. I strained to hear every person we passed, but I couldn't pick up on his voice.

After a minute or so we stopped. The woman seemed to be talking to someone else now. I was too busy listening out for

Pat to hear what she said. Eventually she pulled me forward a step, and a man in front of me spoke.

"What's your name?" He had a strange accent, and his breath was hot and meaty. I recoiled at the smell.

"Joel," I replied, trying my best not to breathe in.

"Okay, Joel. Do your parents have a mobile phone we could call?"

"No."

"No? Come with me and we'll sort you out, then."

My arm was passed off, and I went with Meat-Breath. None of this seemed real. I still couldn't believe that Pat had deserted me, left me vulnerable to attack from scary Southern types. Terrifying thoughts battled each other for supremacy, the honour of being the most horrifying idea to scare me witless. Pat sprawled across a busy London road, cars steaming over his flattened body. Or his corpse dumped in a skip with a meat cleaver stuck in his chest. Or perhaps he had simply been taken hostage by irate terrorists, who according to the Daily Mail were everywhere these days and loved nothing more than a good afternoon session of kidnapping, torturing and dismemberment. I pressed a skinned palm to my head and grimaced.

"Where are we going?" I asked, realising that I was completely disoriented. "I want to wait by the station."

"I'll take you to the information desk," Meat-Breath replied. "They can put out an announcement, see if we can find your parents."

The voices around us grew louder, then a wave of heat and sweat-drenched air engulfed me. We were back inside the station. Meat-Breath pushed into the crowds, his grip tight around my wrist the whole time. I followed without saying a word. Even the pain in my knee seemed distant, like all of this was happening to someone else.

We eventually stopped and Meat-Breath spoke to a bored-sounding guy behind a desk. One of them asked my surname, and I automatically told them. A moment later, a bored-sounding announcement went out across the station.

"Could the parents of Joel Petersen please report to the information desk near the ticket office."

The two men chatted while we waited, and every few minutes the desk guy made another announcement. Somehow I just knew Pat wasn't going to come. After the fifth or sixth effort, Meat-Breath patted me on the shoulder and sighed.

"Right, looks like they're not here. I'll take you down the station, see if we can contact one of your relatives."

"The station? I thought we were at the station?"

"I mean the police station. It's just down the road from here. We'll get you back with your parents in no time."

"Police?" The hollow void in my gut suddenly filled with acid. As dumb as it might sound, I never even thought that Meat-Breath could be a policeman. I knew straight away that I couldn't go with him to the station. If he found out where I lived, they would find Mum. I could end up in jail, with all the murderers and thugs and drug dealers and thieves. They'd probably all pick on me, and call me nicknames even worse than 'Bat Boy'.

"I need to go…to the toilet," I said, hoping I didn't sound too nervous.

"Okay. I'll take you there on the way out."

His hand fastened around my wrist again, and he led me back towards the entrance. I realised how Chops must have felt when he was on his lead, desperate to break loose and be free. I wished he was here right now. He could've launched into a massive barking fit at Meat-Breath and distracted him while I escaped.

Just before we reached the entrance, we turned and pushed our way to the left. Meat-Breath stopped and released my arm.

"I'll just wait here for you," he said.

A door creaked open at my side, and the distant echo of a hand dryer drifted out. I wondered for a moment whether I should bolt out of the station entrance, but I shook the idea off. The place was too crowded, and I'd stand no chance of outrunning anyone outside, on a street I didn't know. Instead, I shuffled through the door.

Every step on the marble floor echoed down the hall that led to the toilets. I could hear more hand dryers, and running taps. My hand traced the left wall, a long row of tiles that were chipped and cracked and covered in paper stickers. The smell of bleach didn't do much to mask the familiar 'public lavatory' stench. I sucked in mini-breaths through my lips and pressed on.

My fingers eventually hit a door, and I pushed my way inside. I only made it two steps before a woman gasped in front of me.

"What do you think you're doing?"

"Oh!" was all I could say. For some reason I just stood there, my mouth agape.

"Well? Get out of here, you little pervert!" Another woman burst into giggles over by a running tap.

"Bless him. He looks a little lost. Men's is across the hall."

I stammered an apology and almost tripped over my own feet on the way out. The door had just shut behind me when an idea formed, and I stopped and turned around. I pushed my way back inside.

"I don't believe it. You can't have gotten lost again, surely!"

"Persistent little sod, isn't he?"

"I'm really sorry," I said, my head lowered. "There's a policeman outside waiting for me, and I need to hide from him."

"You're on the run from the police, eh? What did you do?"

"Probably got caught sneaking into women's rest rooms!"

"Looks more like he's been in a fight, from that bandage on his head."

"No," I said, "nothing like that! I swear!"

"Come on, he's too cute to be a vigilante. Must be mistaken identity, right?"

"Something like that," I replied. The whole of my face right down to my neck was tingling.

"All right, come on, then. Get in a cubicle. But no perving!"

"Can you help me?"

"Help you?"

"I…I can't see. I'm blind."

The toilets fell quiet for a moment. I was kind of used to that reaction whenever I told people. Most of the time they'd have to think about what to say next – to avoid offending me or something, I guess.

"Oh, God, I'm sorry! I didn't know. Don't you have a dog or a cane or anything?"

"I used to have a dog, but he ran off."

"Oh, lord! Come here, I'll help you." A warm but slightly damp hand enclosed mine, and I was led to a nearby cubicle.

I locked the door behind me then took a seat.

"Just wait there, we'll tell you when he's gone."

For five minutes or so, I listened to them whispering. Occasionally the door would swing open. I just stayed silent. Finally, someone knocked on the other side of the cubicle.

"Right, he's gone!"

I unlocked the door and the woman with the warm hand led me back out into the station. I tensed as we pushed our way into the crowds, half-expecting another hand to clamp itself on my shoulder. Luckily, we made it outside without incident.

"Where are you headed to?" the woman asked as we stopped by the side of the entrance.

"Somewhere called Brookfields. I'm going there to live with my Dad."

"Nice. Do you know how to get there?"

"Well, not really. Is it far?"

"No, it's pretty close, just a short bus ride. I can take you to the stop if you like?"

I nodded.

It had been about an hour since Pat and me had split up. I was almost ill with worry, the tightness in my gut spread up my chest. But he hadn't come back to the station, so there seemed little point in hanging around. Maybe if I made it to the pub, he would already be there.

The stop was just around the corner from the station, and the woman waited with me to make sure I got on the right bus.

We chatted while we waited. Her name was Laura, she had a daughter around my age, and she made jam for a living.

"You wanna hear a jam-related joke?" Laura asked. I thought about it for a moment.

"Sure. I don't think I know any jam-related jokes."

"Okay. How does Bob Marley like his donuts?"

"Who's Bob Marley?" There was an awkward silence for about two seconds.

"Are you kidding me? You really don't know who Bob Marley is?"

"Um...Oh, isn't he Scrooge's old partner in A Christmas Carol?"

"No, that's Jacob Marley! Bob Marley was the reggae singer!"

"Oh, right. Yeah, I think I might have heard of him."

"Deary me, the youth of today. I suppose I should be thankful you've even heard of Charles Dickens, right?"

"I like the old classics."

"Just not classic music, I guess. When you see your father, tell him to buy you a Bob Marley CD right away."

She had just launched into a biography of Bob Marley, including a list of his greatest hits that I had to hear no matter what, when the bus turned up.

"Brookfields is the last stop," Laura said as the doors slid open in front of me.

"Thanks for all your help," I said. I offered her a nervous smile.

"Not a problem. Take care of yourself, okay Joel?"

I climbed aboard and was about to find a seat when a sweaty hand caught my arm and pulled me back.

"Where's your ticket?" a gruff voice asked.

"Ticket? I...oh...I don't have one."

"That's two pounds, then."

"But...I'm sorry, I don't have any money on me."

"Then I'm sorry too, but you'll have to get off."

"Hey, wait," Laura said, and she pushed onto the bus behind me. "I'll pay for him." I heard a beep, then the hand released me. A large damp patch was left on my skin. I rubbed my arm and shouted thanks as she jumped off again, a deep burning sensation in my chest. She didn't know me from anyone, yet she'd helped me out and even paid my bus fare, despite my total ignorance of legendary reggae singers.

I padded across the sticky floor and slid into the first seat I found. My entire body ached, my knee worst of all. Just taking the weight off my feet felt amazing, but the lingering tension was still there. Alone again, in the middle of this huge city.

The bus sounded mostly empty. Someone played some tinny music near the back, and a couple chatted about an impending wedding just a few rows behind me. Aside from the occasional snort from the driver, that was it. I tried my best to relax, and rested my head against the window. The vibrations made my skull itch. I leaned forward and dropped my face into my hands.

The ride seemed to take ages. For quite some time I was worried that we'd gone right through Brookfields and were headed back to the station again. I had no two pounds for another fare. Finally, the bus stopped and the engine shut off. I picked myself out of my seat and shuffled to the front.

"Excuse me?" I said as the driver squeezed from his cabin.

"Yeah?"

"Are we in Brookfields?"

"Yeah." He climbed off the bus, and the whole thing trembled. I quickly followed him out into the cold evening air – according to Robot Judi, it was already almost 8pm.

"I need to find a pub," I called out to the driver as he strode away.

"Very funny," he called back without stopping. "Need to drown your sorrows?"

"No, really. I need to find one called Prince Regent."

"Information desk's in the waiting room."

"Where's that?"

"Straight in front of you, kid." I heard him board another bus, then the doors slid shut and he pulled away. I listened to him go, then carefully edged forwards, my hands spread out in front of me.

My fingers brushed ice-cold glass after just a few steps. It took me a while, but I finally found a door – also glass – and pushed it open. I stepped inside. The waiting room was completely silent, and not much warmer than the street outside. I gently closed the door behind me.

"Hello?" My voice seemed somehow shallow, but no one answered me. I tried again, and still no response. I crept further into the room. After just nine steps, my shin caught a solid edge – right on one of my bruises from the bags at the station. I winced and bit my lip.

Further exploration showed that the solid edge was part of a bench, and that was as far back as the room extended. In all, the waiting room was only about 12 paces wide and 20 paces long, with benches lined either side. I found what I presumed was the information desk – a kiosk at the far end, with its shutters drawn.

"Great," I muttered, then I collapsed down onto the hard wooden slabs of the bench beside the window, perhaps a little too enthusiastically. I rested my head back against the freezing pane of glass. Of course, with the combination of exhaustion, stress and frostbite, I had forgotten about the lump there. I yelped in pain, then arched forwards and clutched at my wound.

"Owweee!" My fingers brushed the skin, but even that was

painful. I forced my arms back to my sides and crushed my teeth together. My eyes stung, and tears pushed out from my lower lids and streamed down my cheeks. I pulled my legs up to my chest and clung on to them. With all my might, I wished that Pat would come. I didn't know how he would find me, I just wanted him to walk through the door. I wanted him to tell me everything would be fine. I wouldn't even mind if he ruffled my hair or gave me a noogie.

I held my breath and waited.

Nine

I sat in that room for hours. Occasionally a car would drive by, or a bus would pull up, but just before midnight the street fell completely silent. I shivered on the cold bench and pushed my hands as far into my pockets as I could manage. Then, just as I thought my brain might ice over, I finally heard something on the street outside.

Footsteps!

I sucked in a frosty breath and twisted my head to the side.

"Please, please, please," I whispered. "Come on, Pat. Come on."

A gruff burst of laughter caused my stomach to curl in on itself. I realised the footsteps belonged to more than one person, possibly even more than two. The echo down the deserted street had thrown me. Voices suddenly became clear, all deep, all growly. I could make out three distinct accents.

I lowered my head to my knees and wished that the strangers would keep on walking. They were close now, so close I could make out every word.

"Friggin' selfish old bassart, gimme that! Am dyin' ah thirst!"

"Haven't you had enough?"

"I'll break yer gaddam fingers off! Gimme 'ere!"

They scuffled and swore as they stumbled down the pavement just outside the shelter. I kept my head down and held my breath. They were almost right behind me and one of them belched as they passed the window. I kept repeating in my head, *'KEEP WALKING'*. I had to clench every muscle to stop myself from violently shaking.

My heart almost burst into fleshy confetti when the door of the shelter creaked open. An icy breeze washed over me, but even though my skin felt as if it would shatter beneath my jacket, I didn't dare make a sound. The strangers' mumbled conversation faded and died. I heard their breath, hard and heavy in the silence. Footsteps surrounded me. I held myself completely still, as if doing so somehow made me not exist. Nothing more than a shadow spread across the bench.

"Hey, what the hell's this?" The door slammed shut again, cutting out the draft. I jerked back up straight.

"An intruder!"

"This your kid, Trev? Eh? Marcie drop 'im off for ya to look after the night?" The three men burst into laughter and I dropped my head. A pungent aroma drifted from the three. Not quite an unpleasant scent like body odour, but a kind of musky smell, like they weren't great fans of baths or soap.

"No, can't be Trev's," said another of the men. This one had a thick Indian accent. "He's far too good looking."

"Ye kin do one, Jaz," said the last, the one called Trev. He snorted. "Least a lass lemme close enough ta have ma kids. They'd do a runner just at the look ah ya!"

"So, what you say, lad?" asked the first man. "What brings ya to break into our bungalow? You ain't waiting for a bus, are ya? Cos you might be waiting a while."

"No buses come down here at this time," said Jaz, the Indian. "No one at all comes down here."

I raised my head slightly and cleared my throat.

"I was just hanging around, that's all." Somehow I managed to sound vaguely calm, but I wished more than ever that I had a spare change of underwear.

"What's your story, kid? You a runaway?"

"I'm not running," I said. I shook my head, a little too vigorously. "I'm just looking for my Dad."

"Are you now? And I take it from the fact you've barged your way into our wonderful abode that you ain't found him yet?"

"No...no, not yet."

"Well, lads, what should we do with him? He's snuck in here and taken our best bench." Their footsteps shuffled closer. I crushed myself back against the window. "Bet he's even had a munch on that half-eaten tuna sarnie we was keeping for tonight, eh?"

"No! I don't even like tuna!"

"No? Well, in that case, maybe we'll let you join us, lad. I'm Simon, and this is Jaz and Trev." Simon crashed onto the bench beside me. I released a long, drawn-out breath but my body remained tense.

"His name ain't really Jaz," Trev said. He grunted as he collapsed on the bench opposite. "It's Jazzapezzapetta-whatever. Some frigging foreign balls, ennit."

"Seriously," Jaz said, his tone colder than the gusts outside. "Just shut the hell up, will you?"

Another belch erupted around the waiting room, followed by yet more laughter, the kind of full-on belly-shaking chortles that Santa always let loose with in those old Christmas movies. Except Santa's breath probably never stank of whiskey.

"So, what's your name, kid?" Simon asked.

"Joel."

"Joel, eh. Strange name, that."

I fumbled my hands together and lowered my head. The

silence that followed was unbearable. I could feel their eyes on me, their gaze as sharp as needles. My face was ablaze. Even though they didn't seem to want to rip my limbs off, I couldn't help but think that their mood could quickly change. They were obviously drunk, like Mum used to get all the time. I wondered if they'd try and stop me if I just stood up and ran out.

"You all right? You're damn quiet."

I perked up and my lips parted, but I had no idea what to say. So I just sat there and gawped.

"Should we offer our guest a drink, lads?"

"Here, tek a swig ah that," Trev said. He unscrewed something. Silence. He said, "Gaan on then, tek it!"

"You're blind, aren't you?" Simon said. "Took me a while. Here, hold out your hand."

I obeyed, and a smooth glass bottle without any label was thrust into my hand. I held it away from my body. Even so, the fumes from the contents still drifted to my nostrils. I stuck out my tongue and rasped at the burning sensation at the back of my throat. My reaction earned even more laughter from the others.

"It's very strong, yes?" Jaz said.

"Wugghhhh." I wheezed, coughed and choked like a sixty-a-day smoker. "Whatssat?"

"You don't wanna drink that, believe me," Simon said. I had no problem passing the bottle straight back. "He'll drink anything, Trev. Even bloody mouthwash. Living up to the stereotype, ya might say. Here, have a bit of this instead, smoothest rum yer'll ever taste."

Another bottle was unscrewed, and this time there was no overpowering odour. I sniffed at it just to be sure. The bottle was heavy, the label greasy and peeling away underneath my palm. Even though it didn't burn my nostrils, I immediately wanted to hurl the whole thing across the room, just to get it away. My hands began to tremble, which caused the rum to slosh around inside the glass container. Despite my repulsion, I was too afraid of rejecting their offer, all too aware that their attention was locked onto me. They wouldn't be satisfied until I'd tasted the booze.

I gingerly lifted the neck of the bottle to my lips. My tongue traced the rim, tasting the sweet remnants of the last mouthful. It was sharp. The tip of my tongue tingled immediately.

"Go on kid, take a swig," Simon said. "It ain't poison." His reassurance somehow made me even more nervous. In one terrible moment I felt the label slide away beneath my hands, causing the whole lot to slip from my grasp. The neck banged against my top teeth and my hands flailed, trying to get a grip on the bottle again. Somehow I managed to catch it before it bounced off my lap, and I gripped it to my chest as if it was a live grenade, set to explode at the slightest judder.

"Wohh, wotchit son! 'Spensive stuff, that!"

"S-sorry," I blurted. The bottle was up to my lips again, and the rum filled my mouth until I could take no more. I swallowed it back, then wiped frantically at my mouth with the back of my hand. I thrust the bottle back towards Simon.

My throat was on fire, I was sure of it – someone had tossed a match into my mouth and now great plumes of smoke billowed forth from between my lips and poured from my nostrils. I clawed at my neck, doubled over, and the sound of laughter once again filled the room and drowned out my pitiful wheezing. My fear and revulsion turned to anger. I was so furious that my hands balled into fists, and I began to shake. It took all of my resolve to stay bolted to the bench.

"You all right?" Simon asked, slapping my back.

I nodded and brushed away the spit and tears from my face. I couldn't even tell whether he was genuinely concerned, or just laughing along with the others.

"There ya go, you're a real man now. We can get the party started proper."

The burning in my throat eventually passed, and with it my anger. I sighed and relaxed back against the cold surface of the glass, and the others asked me about how I ended up here.

I cautiously told them our story-so-far, leaving out any details about Mum falling and bashing her head, and us leaving her dead on the floor of her bedroom. Instead, I simply told them about finding the old postcards that Dad had sent.

"They all came from a pub we think's here in Brookfields. A place called Prince Regent."

"The Prince Regent," Jaz repeated. "That isn't far from here. It's one of the oldest pubs in South London, you know."

"Ahh, the Prince!" Trev said, his voice suddenly filled with a nostalgic joy. "'Aven't 'ad a drink inner fer an age!"

"That's cos it's shut down, idiot," Simon said. "For almost as long as we've been living in this dump."

My heart plummeted into my stomach at the news. Although the postcards had been a slim lead at best, actually hearing that the pub had closed down made Dad seem impossibly distant. Our last link had been severed. It reminded me of those detective novels, where the PI finally tracks down the only witness after countless car chases and gunfights, only for them to be gunned down right before his eyes.

"Any idea where my Dad could have bought the postcard?" I asked, without too much self-pity in my tone.

"You can't buy these things, not in any shops. Only geezer who dished these out was the ol' landlord, Davey. Your Dad must've been a regular."

Quite a regular, considering how many of the postcards he'd sent. I slumped back in my seat and let out a tiny moan. Not only were my chances of finding Dad bleak, so were any chances of finding Pat again. I wondered if I should just turn myself in to the police, and be done with it. Then I tried one final, hopelessly optimistic question.

"Do you think I'd be able to find Davey and ask him about Dad?"

"Could be, but yer talking a while back now. Pub's been closed a few years."

"Davey still lives there though," Jaz said. "You could go and ask him. If your father went there often, he might still be in touch. He was pretty close with his regulars."

Suddenly, a beacon of hope was lit again.

Okay, so even if Davey did remember our father, there was practically no chance they would still be friends – but practically no chance was still a chance.

"Can take you to the pub now if yer like," Simon said. "Davey should be there."

"You don't think it's too late? What if we wake him?"

"Nahh, he'll have some of his clients round, no doubt."

"I thought the pub was closed?" I asked, suddenly confused.

"S'not a pub no more," Trev said, hocking up a throatful of phlegm. I shuffled my feet back under the bench, hoping his spray hadn't caught me.

"Yeah," Simon said, "Davey's turned it into some kinda gambling den. That's why we don't go round no more, see – no cash to gamble with. So, you wannus to take ya?"

Immediately I was suspicious. I ran their offer through my head a couple of times, then wondered what other choice I had. If I didn't want to spend the night in a bus shelter, this was my only shot.

"Only if you don't mind."

"Not at all. We don't 'ave any functions or parties to attend the night, eh lads?"

"Just as well," Jaz said, "my tux is in the cleaners."

I rose from the bench, then we stepped out of the bus shelter and made our way down the freezing cold, desolate London street, headed for the Prince Regent.

Part Three... Unfortunate Circumstances

Ten

The time was almost 'eleven pee em' when we arrived at the Prince Regent, and the weather had taken a violent turn. A fierce wind gushed down the streets as if fleeing for its life. I was glad that Simon let me hang off his arm, as a number of times the gales spread my jacket like heavy, lifeless wings, and I was terrified I'd be carried off.

"Here we are," Simon said, his voice suddenly hushed. I could barely hear him over the wind. "Just as lovely as ever."

"How does it look?" I asked.

"Like a condemned old bordello that never got knocked down. Few more of the windows are boarded up than last time I was here. Actually, all of 'em are boarded up now. And looks like someone added a charming bit of graffiti to the front door. I won't even repeat it, for fear of shocking your poor, innocent little mind."

"You're sure he still lives there?"

"Entrance is 'round the back," Simon said, and he led me there. The concrete underfoot soon turned to gravel, and my left shoulder brushed up against some old, chalky wall that crumbled at my touch. A short distance on we turned a corner. Finally, some shelter from the wind. "Just here."

Four heavy knocks against a thick wooden door. We waited until I was certain the occupants were either asleep or absent. None of us moved or even spoke and Simon didn't attempt to knock again. I had just built up the confidence to say something when the door in front of us rattled in its frame, and

I heard a bolt being forced back on the other side. This was followed by another, and then rapid pounding that sounded like someone trying to kick the door open.

"Is he scared someone's going to break in?" I asked. Simon let out a tiny chortle.

"He just don't want any unwelcome visits from the local constabulary is all."

Finally, the door swung inwards and a wave of hot air rushed past us, taking the edge off the chill. I immediately longed to be inside. I imagined one of those old-fashioned places with a blazing fire in one corner, and a dog curled up asleep beside it. His owner relaxed in a rocking chair with a pipe and slippers.

"Frig do you want?" asked the man stood in the doorway. He had a strong cockney twang, although his voice wasn't quite as gruff as Simon's or Trev's.

"Not the way ta greet old friends, Davey, is it?" Simon replied. "And watch yer frigging mouth, there's a kid present."

"I can see that, you nonce. What you doing bringing scrags round here? He's not Trev's, is he?"

"Too good looking for that," Jaz said, and Trev launched into his usual tirade of abuse.

"So, come on then," Davey said after the obscenities died down. "What the hell do you want? I've got games going on in here."

Simon gave a fake, almost threatening guffaw. There was a short silence, during which I swear I heard a distant scream, followed by the screeching of tyres across a road.

"We're just 'ere on a favour, mate. This kid's looking for 'is Dad, an' all he knows is the guy used to come here. Sent 'im a huge pile of those postcards ya used to keep."

"Postcards? Bloody hell. Your name isn't...Joe, by any chance, is it?"

"Joel," I said, and my heart almost skipped a beat. How the hell did he know that?

"Joel, that's right. Okay, I'll take this one off your hands, fellas."

"Cheers Davey," Simon said. "Yer a star. I'll leave 'im in yer capable hands, then. Careful with him though, the kid can't peep nothing."

Simon gently pushed me forwards, and my feet moved almost automatically.

Jaz called out a quick goodbye as I stepped over the threshold into the boarded-up carcass of the Prince Regent. Trev added his own parting sentiments, although they were incomprehensible.

I turned to thank them, but another hand grabbed hold of my shoulder and pulled me inside.

"Take care then, lad," Simon said. "And merry Christmas!" Before I could reply, the door was slammed shut.

"Follow me, Joel." There was a hint of smugness in Davey's tone, and my stomach tensed again. I was pulled along a narrow corridor. My feet scuffed across the thick carpet, and my shoulders occasionally brushed the flaky walls either side. The air in here was a cocktail of various scents, from old smoke and ash to stale and rotten food. It lingered like a thick fog, as if it seeped from living pores in the walls. I held my breath as best I could, trying not to suck in the toxins for the fear they'd choke me.

"So...do you remember my Dad? His name's Darrel. Darrel Petersen."

"Remember him?" Davey snorted. "You could say that.

There's someone here I think you're gonna want to see. Well, not see. You know what I mean."

"Is it Dad? Is he here?" I could barely contain my sudden excitement.

"Look, kid, no more questions. That crap drives me crazy. *Mind your head* here." His warning tone stunned me into silence, and I was so shaken that I didn't heed his words. A moment later we turned right, and my forehead smacked straight into some kind of wooden beam.

Davey squeezed my arm and made a 'that-must-have-hurt' blowing sound.

"I told you to watch your bloody head!"

"It's okay," I muttered, clutching my already-bandaged head in my hand. At least now I'd have a matching front-lump to go with the one at the back.

I was slowly led down a set of creaky stairs. The stench did not reach down here, although the tang of musty, humid air had replaced it.

On the way down, my fingers traced the wall, a misshapen layer of cold and dripping stone, smooth to the touch. I could hear men talking and shouting somewhere below, and the clinking of glasses.

Hesitancy crept over me again, a terrible dread that perhaps Davey was lying. All the secrecy had me concerned that he'd never actually met our Dad at all, and this was all just some sinister charade. But why else would he take me in? From all the gambling talk, he could've been some kind of gangster. Was I planning on using me for child labour, chaining me up like a slave in his basement and forcing me to fetch him and his criminal gang food and drinks? Would I eat out of a bowl like a dog, and go to the bathroom right there in the corner? Maybe

I'd finally be released when I was too old or weak to be of any use, and I'd spend the rest of my days clawing through garbage for food and running scared from the sunlight that burned my translucent skin.

I pulled back against Davey's grip, trying to halt our descent into the creaking bowels of the broken-down old pub. Davey stopped on the step below me.

"Come on, shift a leg."

"Uh…why…why are we going down here?"

"Hey, don't worry. We're just playing cards down here, that's all. Like I said, there's someone you'll wanna see." We stood there in silence for a moment, then Davey added: "You're free to go if you want. You wanna leave?"

I shifted my weight from one leg to the other. The step beneath me creaked. This was definitely my best chance of finding Dad – what would I do if I left? Sleep in the bus shelter every night?

I thought it over, my bottom lip clenched between my teeth.

"Okay." I sighed and nodded.

Davey squeezed my arm, and we continued to the bottom of the staircase.

The floor of the basement was covered in wooden boards, but they didn't protest at our weight as loudly as the stairs had. It was obvious from the echo of our footsteps that the room was quite wide but not tall, and I felt sure that if I reached upwards I would touch the ceiling.

The air was almost uncomfortably hot now, yet still damp, as if we'd descended into some strange tropical jungle. The cocktail of smells had made way for the bitter odour of smoke instead.

We turned back around the staircase and headed towards

the other men. Their conversation was now clearly audible. The smell of smoke grew thicker.

"You got nothing, ya lying git. I can see it in those twinkle friggin' eyes of yours."

"If you're so sure, frig-face, why don't you call me?"

The other men all cackled and threw in their own words of encouragement or abuse. At an estimate, I would place six of them there in all. They were so engrossed that none of them appeared to notice us stop beside the table.

Someone else noticed us, though.

"Joel! Holy crap, Joel!"

"Pat?" I couldn't believe it. My brother ran up to me and crushed me in his arms, and I hugged him right back. Tears sprang from my eyes.

"What happened to you? I waited for ages outside the station, but you never came back!"

"Gah, I'm really sorry. This bloody kid nicked my wallet out of my pocket. I ran after him, but he went down this alley and when I followed him, these huge guys jumped out at me. There must've been ten or twenty of 'em. Big sods. I fought them off best I could, but one of 'em got me good. Then, to cap it off, I realised I was completely lost. Took me ages to get back."

"Really?" The huge gang of thugs part sounded like an embellishment, but I didn't question it. I was just so glad to have him back. "Are you okay?"

"Just a few bumps and scrapes, that's all. Gonna need a bandage, then we'll be all matching, eh?"

"Have you been here long?"

"Just a couple of hours, I think. I've been asleep. I waited outside the station for ages, but you must've already left."

"What is this?" one of the card players said, interrupting our reunion. "Is it kiddies' night in here or something, eh?"

"Yeah, who's this new sprog?" asked another of the men – the one who had called his friend a frig-face.

"He's Darrel Petersen's other lad," Davey replied.

"Darrel Petersen had two kids?" said another, evidently taken aback. "I didn't even know he had one till this lad showed up."

"Neither did I. But here they are, paying us a visit, and I reckon we should make them feel right at home, eh?" Again there was something about Davey's tone that unsettled me. The other men talked amongst themselves in hushed voices.

"Uhh, we don't wanna be any trouble or owt," Pat said. He cleared his throat with a weighty cough.

"No trouble at all," Davey said, and his hand clamped down on my shoulder. "In fact, you two could even help us out with a little problem of ours. Whaddaya say?"

"Problem? What kinda problem?"

"A problem with your father. You see, he owes me a small pile of cash at the moment, and he doesn't seem too keen to pay up. He keeps putting me off with excuses. It's starting to wear pretty thin, to be perfectly honest. But now that you two have landed on my doorstep, perhaps he'll be a bit more willing to give up the dosh, eh?" He cackled like some kind of sinister old warlock.

"Really?" Pat stammered. "He owes you cash? Well, I'm not sure we can really help, to be honest. He really ain't actually our Dad at all, actually. He's more of a…distant uncle. We were just in the area and thought we'd check him out, yeah?"

The grip on my shoulder tightened, and Davey's fingernails

dug deep into my skin through my jacket. I winced and tried to pull away, but he held firm.

"I know that's just a lie, Pat. Don't worry though, we're a hospitable bunch. As soon as this little matter's resolved you can be on your merry way with your father, and we'll all be good friends, eh. In fact, by coming here you may well have saved your Dad's thumbs, know what I mean?"

Davey gave me a final squeeze, then released me. I clutched my shoulder. Fat drops of sweat trickled down my forehead and seeped into my eyes until they stung. My heart stampeded in a panic around my chest. With every frantic beat my ears throbbed, filling with blood, until a dull ringing clouded out the voices surrounding me. Pat continued to protest, but it was all so distant now.

"Just sit down there and be quiet," Davey told us, and we ended up on what felt like a battered old mattress in the corner furthest from the stairs. The edge of a spring poked up through the worn material and jabbed into my leg, but I didn't dare make a sound or even move. Davey's footsteps trailed back to the table, roughly twenty feet away, and the men resumed their card game.

"Frigging great, this is," Pat hissed. He shifted beside me. "You were right. This was a stupid bloody idea. These guys are dodgy as hell. They keep talking about all this shady stuff, summat about cargo they're gonna pick up. I think they're planning on nicking summat big."

"Why does that even bother you?" I asked. "You used to work for people like them yourself."

"Not like these guys. They're...I don't know, there's just something wrong about them. We should've just stayed home. Even with Mum stinking up the place, at least we could've been playing Mortal Kombat and eating pizza and…crap, anything but sitting in some frigging basement with these morons." His remark was followed up with several other words, all of which contained four letters.

I leaned forwards and buried my head between my knees.

"Maybe it'll be okay. Maybe Dad will just give him whatever he owes, and take us away."

"Maybe. Or maybe we should just get the hell out of here ourselves."

"I don't think Davey's going to just let us stroll out. There's no point in escaping anyway, we'll have no chance of finding Dad then. And you heard what Davey said, that thing about us saving Dad's thumbs."

I wrung my hands together, shivering. What would he actually do to Dad's thumbs if we escaped? Would he simply break them, or would he cut them off whole? Or perhaps just slice them off at the knuckle. That would definitely still get his point across.

"So you wanna just sit here? The guy's nuts! What's to say he won't torture us instead? He probably gets off on it. And what happens if Dad doesn't pay up, huh? This is his mess, and we'll be the ones who get our kneecaps bashed in! Honestly, who'd lend money off this guy? He's a complete arsehole."

I suddenly realised that we knew almost entirely nothing about our father, yet we'd travelled almost the entire length of the country to track him down, just expecting him to take us in. What if he was no better than Mum – or even worse than her, if that was possible? My mind fogged and I realised we may have just made the biggest mistake of our lives.

Eleven

Pat moped and kicked his heels against the mattress while Davey and his goons played poker. They were still busy discussing some kind of 'cargo' that they were going to collect, but I couldn't make out most of the conversation as they kept their voices hushed. Well, except for those heated moments when they screamed abuse and threats at each other.

My mind wandered, imagining the kinds of horrible things those men might do to us if Dad really didn't pay up. For history studies last year, I did some research into punishment in medieval times. There were some pretty grisly methods to get confessions out of prisoners. Every single instrument of torture flashed through my mind, from the metal combs used to peel back flesh to the hugely complex machines that could bend a man until his bones cracked apart and his limbs were torn from his body. All the while, I listened for a quick movement, half-expecting a set of hands to grab hold of me and drag me, kicking and screaming, into some kind of sordid torture den.

After some horrible length of time, one of the chairs in front of us clattered to the ground and the men once again screamed at each other, cramming in more swear words than I could keep up with.

"What the frig is that!"

"What the frig is what?"

"I frigging saw Natt slip something from his jacket pocket! You hiding cards in there, you cheating frigger?"

"The hell you talking about? It's my inhaler, you daft git!"

"Yeah? Well, let's frigging see it then!"

"Calm the frig down, will you, it was just the guy's frigging inhaler."

"Yeah, see? This frigging basement's smoky as hell with all you frigging morons sat around with your frigging cigars!"

"Hey, watch it!"

"He's just grumpy cos he's gotta freeze his arse off on that boat tomorrow."

"Well, wouldn't you be? Two whole weeks with that fat frigger there, snoring all night and picking his arse all day!"

"Frig you pal, it ain't exactly a paradise cruise sailing with you neither! Makes me nauseous watching you heave over the side every five minutes, and your endless bitching about everything." The man put on a whiny voice. "Ugh, this food's disgusting. Baked beans again, how disgusting. Haven't we got any smoked salmon and creme de broolay?"

"Bollocks, I don't talk like that! And what's wrong with having standards, eh? Just cos you'd happily spoon lard in your fat frigging face three meals a day!"

The argument continued for some time. We sat there in stunned silence, taking in every word. Eventually Pat turned and whispered in my ear. "These dudes are nuts. Totally nuts."

I could only nod, and pray that they didn't all pull out guns and empty them across the table at each other. Or if there was a massacre, that we wouldn't be caught in the crossfire.

I scooted across the mattress until my back was pressed against the wall, then hitched my knees up to my chest.

"What you laughing for, Rob? You think it's funny? Why don't you go on the damn trip instead, see how jolly you're feeling then?"

"Try and make me, moron."

More chairs scraped back across the wooden floorboards.

Pat's hand circled my arm and clenched tight. I braced myself, my muscles tensed, ready to propel myself out of the path of bullets if necessary.

"Hey, hey, hey!" shouted Davey over the top of them all. "Why must our gatherings always descend into infantile bickering! Shut the frig up, the lot of ya! You're giving me a migraine!" The noise petered out until all I could hear was a chorus of raspy breaths. "That's better. Now come on, let's have a little Christmas cheer, eh? Natt, pick up your cards and finish the game."

"What's the point, everyone's bloody seen 'em now."

"Well, whose fault is that? Come on, we only saw one, and we'll all pretend we never noticed."

The men took their seats again and play resumed, as did their conversation about the cargo.

The topic eventually changed to a girl called Diane, who apparently has the biggest puppies in London, although she doesn't let them out much, which seemed to disappoint the group. Well, no wonder they were so big, if they don't get any proper exercise. I used to take Chops out at least twice a day, just so he could run about and do his business.

"I really thought they were gonna kill each other then," Pat whispered, and he finally released my arm. My skin tingled where his fingers had dug in.

"Me too. I really wish we'd never come here, Pat."

"You and me both. Don't worry, though. I'm thinking up a plan."

Knowing that Pat was working on a plan actually made me more nervous. So far, our plans had got us into nothing but trouble. But before I had a chance to get more details, heavy footsteps approached our corner.

"Hello boys," Davey said, and he stopped at the foot of the mattress. "You two look cosy. Still sitting tight?"

"Have you heard from our Dad?" Pat's voice was drenched in loathing.

"Don't you worry yourself." Davey turned and strode back to the table, leaving us sitting in silence. I considered asking Pat about his plan, but something – possibly cold fear – stopped me.

The group eventually finished their poker game and said their goodbyes to Davey, then headed back up the stairs.

"Natt, Rob, I'll see you at the port tomorrow at six," Davey said on the way up. "Don't be late again, or I'll feed you to the frigging sharks."

Davey followed them upstairs and I heard the complicated procedure of bolt-sliding and lock-releasing at the front door. I puffed out a breath and rubbed the back of my neck with tensed fingers. Pat's hand went to my shoulder.

"Don't worry, it's just Davey now."

The other men had departed, and Davey was bolting the door up again.

I frowned. "He probably worries me most of any of them."

"But this is our chance, man. D'you remember that film, Nazi Death Squad?"

"What?" A psychopathic loan shark/torturer/murderer was on his way down to the basement, probably clutching a shotgun, or at the very least a claw hammer, and my brother wanted to discuss cheesy action films that we'd watched together as kids.

"Nazi Death Squad," he repeated, "you remember it?"

"Yeah, I remember it. So what?"

The film had been one of those ridiculous low-budget horrors we'd sat through at 3am when Mum was passed out. This one involved a Nazi platoon brought back from the dead by a mad scientist, who sent them out in flying saucers to conquer the galaxy. My overriding memory of the film, apart from the scene where the zombie Nazis took on a group of shiny plastic Martians, was the terrible acting. Even when confronted with a whole legion of flying undead fascists, the actors had delivered their lines like they were reading out their shopping lists.

"You remember the scene where Captain Ringo and Barbara escape from the cell on the Nazi spaceship?"

"You can't be serious!"

"Come on, it's worth a go! This guy's a frigging nut job!"

The door at the top of the stairs creaked open, then more creaks echoed down as our captor descended the rickety staircase. I dug my nails into the dusty mattress and sucked in deep breaths of the smoky air.

"Come on, Joel, this is it. You be Barbara, right? It'll work, I promise!"

I dropped to my side and clutched my belly while Pat called out to Davey. I had no real time to think about what I was doing, and if I did, I probably wouldn't have gone along with Pat's absurd plan. But it was too late. Davey shuffled towards us across the dusty floor.

"What's up now, huh?"

"It's my brother, he's sick. Please, can you take him to the bathroom?"

"You what? He was fine two minutes ago. You having me on?"

"No, I swear it! He's mumbling summat, saying he's gonna

puke all over the place. He gets like this whenever he's nervous." For a moment all I could make out was Pat's frantic breath, and Davey muttering a string of curses.

"Come on then, get up." Davey grabbed my arm and I crawled up onto my knees and staggered to my feet, all the while moaning and grunting and squeezing my gut. Not much acting was actually required – my heart pounded violently and my stomach was so crushed up that I really did feel sick.

"Hey," Davey said, leading me towards the staircase. "You really gonna yack? If you throw up across my – "

At that moment, a mighty roar erupted from behind us. Davey suddenly staggered forwards, grunting and yelling in surprise, before he crashed against his poker table. I heard chips and cards scatter across the floor as Pat bellowed in triumph. I was pushed to the ground amidst the chaos but immediately scrambled to my feet, wincing at the scrapes across my palms. With those two struggling, all I could do was stand there and wonder what the hell to do next. In the film, Barbara had saved Captain Ringo by shooting the Nazi guards with a laser gun, but that didn't really help me much.

"Quick," Pat yelled, "I got him! Run!" Davey was spluttering and wheezing, as if Pat was crushing his neck. The pair of them danced madly around the basement, slamming into everything they could. I hesitated for a second. The last thing I wanted to do was split up with Pat again, especially if it meant leaving him alone with Davey. They crashed into something to my right, and the sound of shattering glass filled the basement.

"Run, Joel!"

"I'll get help," I yelled back, then I turned and sprinted for the staircase. I only made it a few steps before my feet caught a duffel bag. Once again I crashed to the solid wooden floor, only this time my shoulder twisted back in the socket. I screamed and rolled onto my side, my hand crushed against the throbbing joint.

The struggle continued behind me. Furniture clattered to the ground with a host of frantic grunts and snorts. They stumbled in my direction, quickly building up speed, and I ground my teeth together and pushed myself up onto my knees using my good shoulder. With an agonised wail I made it to my feet and scrambled out of their way, just before they stumbled into me. A stray arm knocked me to the side, but I righted myself and staggered to the bottom of the stairs.

My knees were bruised and sore. My shoulder ached as if someone had slammed me with a cricket bat. Still, I powered up the steps, my legs burning from the effort. Those stairs sounded as if they would give way any second, but the thought of Davey shaking off Pat and chasing after me was far more terrifying than any chance I might collapse through the ageing wood.

"What the hell are you doing! Gerrof, you little bastard!"

Another thunderous crash, followed by wood splintering apart. I slowed for the briefest of moments, praying that Pat was okay. I'd never felt so useless in my entire life. What the hell was I doing, abandoning him like this? If something happened to him, I knew I'd hate myself forever – a million times worse than I already did for leaving Mum lifeless on her bedroom floor. But then Pat's voice rang out once more, and I whimpered with relief.

"Keep going, Joel! Get help!"

After eighteen steps I reached the top and turned into the hallway. My fingertips traced the walls either side as I staggered towards the front door. The shouting continued below, but I tried to concentrate on getting the hell out of this place and finding someone – anyone – who could help us. I came to the door and reached out, feeling my way across the surface until I found the edge. I ran my fingers up and grabbed the two bolts that were locked in place.

"Joel!"

It was Davey. His voice boomed out from below.

"Joel, come back down here! Now!"

My hands trembled, but I managed to curl them around the bolt handles. I tried to force them both back at once but they were too stiff, so I let go of one and gripped the other as tight as I could in both hands. I heaved it with all my might. The bolt shifted a fraction, barely even noticeable. I sucked in another breath. Try again on the count of three. A bitter wail escaped me, and I threw my weight against it once more. This time the bolt shot backwards. I collapsed against the wall and my shoulder wrenched and exploded in agony. Tears of desperation welled in my eyes.

One bolt remained.

My hands went to the second bolt, but the strength had drained from my arms. Useless and pathetic. I kicked the door and howled. Got to do this. Got to do this for Pat. My fingers shifted, then I braced myself and...

Someone pounded three times on the other side of the door.

I almost fell backwards with shock.

Some men could be heard out on the doorstep, their voices only just audible over the gales that whistled past. Some of Davey's goons, come back for some reason.

They pounded on the door again and I backed away, then turned and sprinted down the hallway. The door to the basement came up on my right but I flew past it, my arms spread before me.

I staggered through an open doorway into another room. Only now did I notice the smell again – the stench of rotting food, which seemed to come from somewhere in here. I clamped my lips closed and held my breath. The carpet beneath my feet was shaggy, like I was stood on the back of a giant dog, and the air was almost unbearably hot.

I pushed on, desperate to find another way out. I touched the wall and quickly followed it along until I reached the corner. My leg knocked against something hard – some kind of bin, by the feel. This was where the stench came from. I staggered to the side, my palm back on the wall. After a few steps, the wall fell away and my hand slapped something hard and rough. I felt a sliver of a breeze on my palm. A window! But there was no glass, only wood. The whole thing was covered in thick boards that were nailed in place. I pushed one, then threw myself against it, but it didn't even tremble. A whimper escaped my lips as I beat my fists against the rough surface.

"There's got to be a way out!"

Behind me, I heard a creaking sound from the basement steps. Someone was headed up. The pounding continued from the front door, more frantic now.

I rushed back across the room and slipped through to the hallway, then paused by the side of the basement door.

"Frigging kids," I heard from below. "I'll skin the pair of 'em."

I almost crumpled right there, and had to extinguish a sob before it left my lips and betrayed me. The footsteps headed this way belonged to Davey.

Pat was still somewhere down below, now still and silent.

The grunts and curses came closer, until Davey was only a couple of steps away. My lips curled into a snarl, and my face flushed.

Not gonna get away with this!

The second he reached the top, I burst around the corner and threw myself at him. My flailing arms caught him in his chest and pushed him backwards and he let out a startled shriek. Fingers clawed at my jacket, but slipped away. I felt myself tumble after him, and in a desperate attempt to stop myself, I reached back and made a grab for the door frame. I just caught the edge and managed to hold on, despite the pain that shot through my shoulder. Davey tumbled away below me, the stairs crunching under his weight.

I stood at the top for a moment, struggling for breath. Had I really just done that? Davey hit the basement floor, then there was only silence.

A violent slam against the front door knocked me from my stupor.

"Pat," I called. No response. I jerked my way back down into the basement, somehow without losing my footing, and stopped two steps from the bottom.

"Pat, where are you?" Still nothing. I slid down onto the next step and brushed something with my foot. Davey was sprawled out just ahead. I tried to edge my way past his portly frame, without stepping on him. "Pat? Come on, Pat, say something!"

"Unnnghhh..."

The noise came from Davey. I felt part of him shift beside my leg and I propelled myself away, back into the basement. My heart almost burst clean out of my chest, but somehow I managed not to scream.

"Pat, where are you? I know you're here!"

Something moved, out in the middle of the room. I twisted towards the sound, then crept closer. Broken glass crunched beneath my trainers. A groan, just a few feet ahead.

"Pat?"

"Bloody hell. Joel?"

"Pat, thank god!" I crouched and found him, spread out on the floor. I helped him sit up. "Are you okay?"

"Blehhh. My head is wrecked, man."

"Come on, we've got to go!"

"Wait... Where's Davey?"

"I knocked him down the stairs. Come on, he's waking up!"

"You did what?"

He staggered to his feet and we hurried to the staircase. Davey let out another groan from the bottom. I could hear him moving, thrashing out with his arms and legs. The thought of stepping over him terrified me, but we had no choice.

"Bloody hell," Pat said. "You did that?"

"Let's just go!"

Pat went first, his hand tight around my wrist to make sure I followed. My foot brushed Davey again, and this time his arm came up and his fingers clawed at my jeans.

"Frigging... kid!"

"Aaaarghh!" I kicked his arm away and jumped up the steps, almost barging Pat over. We clambered up them as fast as we could, two at a time, even with my legs burning and my shoulder in agony, as if the bone had snapped and the jagged edges were tearing into my flesh. Behind us, Davey's curses were blocked out by a shrill ringing sound. His mobile phone. Probably the goons at the front door, who continued to pound against the other side.

"Crap, where do we go now?"

"This way," I said. I pointed right, into the room with the boarded-up window. Pat led us there.

"Bugger, the stupid window's all shut up!"

"Isn't there another way out?" I asked. "Another door, or anything at all?"

"Nothing. Just some stairs going up. Oh, crap, you hear that?" Unfortunately, I had heard that. The basement stairs creaked again, one at a time. Davey was on his way up for the second time.

"Let's try upstairs," I hissed, and Pat didn't hesitate. He almost yanked my arm free as he charged across the room.

"Frigging kids, I'll bite your heads off," Davey screamed behind us. I didn't doubt him for a second.

We bounded up the stairs, which were covered in a thick carpet just like the rest of the room. I almost tripped with every step, the hairy tufts grabbing at my ankles as if they were trying to stop us.

At the top, we burst down another hallway.

Pat tried every door we passed, but each room was the same as the last.

"All the windows are boarded up!" he gasped. "This place is like a frigging prison!"

"Try the next one!"

"That's it, man, that's all the rooms up here! There's nowhere left to go!"

Downstairs, I heard the second bolt of the front door pulled back. A moment later, voices and footsteps crossed the hallway beneath us. Davey was in heated debate with his lackeys. They started up the stairs behind us, the stairs we had just climbed.

"They're coming," I said. Pat squeezed my arm.

"Looks like we're dead, then. Bloody hell. I never thought it'd end like this. If anything, I thought Mum would be the one that killed me."

The footsteps stopped at the end of the hallway. Davey's voice rang out again:

"There they are! I'm gonna scoop their frigging eyes out with my bare hands!"

"Oh, crap!" Pat hissed, and he pushed me back with his arm. "I don't believe it. It's him!"

"What?"

"It's him, Joel. It's the fat man. It's the frigging fat man. He's here with Davey."

The fat man. I had no idea how he'd found us, or what he was doing here, but this time there was no escape.

Twelve

"Just stay back," Pat told me. I nodded, my body tensed as if I were a wildcat, ready to strike at anything that came near me. Davey and the fat man crossed the hall towards us, their footsteps horribly loud against the wooden boards. They argued the whole way.

"I could've broke my back cos of these little sods! I can feel my vertebrae crunching as I walk!"

"You must've scared them to death!"

Something was wrong. I could hear three sets of feet, not just two, and now three voices that shouted over each other. Pat's fingernails dug into my arm, and he gasped.

"Holy crap," he whispered.

"What is it? Pat, what's going on?"

"Joel...our Dad's here."

I wasn't sure I'd heard him right. The three men stopped a little way ahead, then one of them stepped forwards until he was almost within touching distance, his footsteps light across the carpet. The argument had ended. My entire body trembled, my skin hot and itchy.

"Pat? Joel?"

I instantly knew it was him. Even though I'd never heard his voice before – a soothing rasp that could almost have belonged to an ageing rock star – it was obvious. His breath came fast and heavy, as if he'd just run a marathon. I simply stood there, frozen.

"I can't believe you're here," Dad said.

He took another step forward and I felt his breath brush through my hair. His hand went to my cheek, the rough and callused tips of his fingers tracing tender circles across my skin.

His touch snapped me from my daze, and I launched myself at him, wrapping my arms around his torso and burying my face in the softness of his shirt. He hugged me back with such ferocity, and even though my fingers barely met around his back, I tried my best to match his strength. A faint scent of deodorant reached my nostrils. I relished it, sucking in greedy breaths until my chest ached.

I could have stayed like that for hours, but his hand went to my head and ruffled the patches of hair that stuck free from my bandages, then he pulled me back again, as if to examine me.

I lowered my head in embarrassment. "Hi," was all I could say, a sheepish grin stretched across my face.

"You're a hell of a handsome lad, eh. You too, Pat. Growing into quite the man, I see."

"Yeah, I guess so," was all Pat said in reply. He sounded stunned, or perhaps just exhausted.

"I'm sorry for everything you've been through. I…I still can't believe I'm actually looking at you both right now."

"Who the hell is the fat guy?" Pat asked abruptly. "What's he doing here? Doesn't he work for Matty's brother?"

"Matty's brother?" the fat man repeated. His voice was nasal, as if he had a grape stuffed up each nostril. He sounded just as confused as I felt. "No, I work for your father."

"What are you talking about? You've been following us all the way from up north!"

"Explanation on the way back," Dad said. "I promise. Come on, let's get out of here."

134

"We can just go?" Pat asked, his voice drenched in suspicion. Davey grunted.

"You still owe me for my back, *Darrel*."

"You got your money, you leech. We're even."

"Even? Maybe we'd be even if I took a pipe to your bloody spine!"

"Try it and see what happens."

Silence. Davey grunted again.

"Have a good day. Please frig off out of my house, the lot of you. And if I ever see you again – either of you – I'm going to tear off your ears and use 'em as novelty ashtrays. Got it?"

I figured that parting comment was aimed at me and Pat. I had no intention of going anywhere near this place again, so I just nodded as we pushed past.

When we finally emerged from the Prince Regent, the breeze that hit my face was a blessed relief. The feeling didn't last long, though. I was so disoriented that my stomach lurched, sending a nauseating tremor right up my throat. For one terrible moment I thought I would puke, so I bent forwards and clutched my knees while my chest heaved. Pat called my name, then I felt his hand on my back. The feeling passed almost as quickly as it started. I stayed locked in place for a while, just to make sure, then I straightened and spat out the bitter saliva that had collected in my mouth.

"You all right?" Pat asked.

"I think so. Urgh, just felt a bit off."

We rounded the pub and started down the road, the same one I'd come down the night before. My legs were still shaking so we kept to a gentle pace, with Pat on my arm as usual.

"I'm sorry if Davey scared you," Dad said. "I came as soon as I heard you were there."

"Scared us?" Pat said with a snort. "He only bloody kept us prisoner in his basement. I thought he was gonna shoot us and bury us down there."

"And he said he would cut off your thumbs," I added.

To my surprise, Dad just laughed.

"Did he now? He's just a load of hot air, that man. I wouldn't worry about anything he says. So, what the hell brings you both down to London?"

"We just wanted to see you," Pat said. "We found these postcards back home, in a shoe box. So we thought we'd try tracking you down."

The postcards exchanged hands.

"Oh, these old things," Dad said with a chuckle. "I sent these years back, not long after...not long after I came to London. Your mother never showed you these before?"

"Nope. She hid 'em away, in her cupboard."

"Figures. I never got replies to anything I sent." A dejected sigh. That was when Dad asked the question that I had been dreading, the question I hoped would somehow never come.

"So, how is your Mum?"

There must have been something in the painful silence that followed which told him all was not well.

"First, who's that guy?" Pat asked to change the subject. I figured he was talking about the fat man, who kept pace just behind us.

"His name's Leo. He's a good man, worked for me for a few years now. A little quiet maybe, but he gets the job done."

That only raised further questions, but we were already at Dad's car. Pat helped me into the back and I settled into the tough fabric seat while Pat and slid in beside me. Dad and Leo got in the front, Leo in the driver's seat.

I groped over my shoulder until I found the seatbelt and slipped it into place.

My throat was still parched, all scratchy and sore whenever I spoke or took a deep breath. As well as that, my stomach was still unsettled. I realised I hadn't had anything to eat or drink in hours. A deep craving for Dr Pepper and pizza overcame me, and I had to push back any thoughts of food in case my stomach digested itself and all the surrounding organs.

For a few seconds the engine stuttered, then exploded into life with a roar and a *ka-thunk*.

"So," Pat said, "you sent this guy up north to try and find us or summat?"

"No, I'd already found you. I got a tip-off last week, and Leo was just checking it out for me."

"A tip-off? What you talking about?"

"Just a rumour about where you were living, that's all. I put out a few feelers a long time ago, and one of them finally came good."

"You're making no sense."

"Don't worry about it. What's important is that I found you at last."

"So Leo was basically spying on us for you?"

"Not spying, that's the wrong word. He was just sort of watching you from afar."

"Surely that's the same as spying?"

"Well, maybe, I guess."

"But in the park," I said, unable to stay silent any longer. "Dad, he tried to grab me...and Chops – what happened to Chops?"

"Take it Chops is your dog?" Leo said. I'd almost forgotten he was even there.

"Yes. He was gone when I woke up."

"My job was just to make sure you were both well. I followed you to the park that morning, watched you fall asleep while your dog…Chips?"

"Chops, it's Chops."

"Chops. Was maybe twenty minutes or so when three lads, all about Pat's age, came wandering along. Chops ran up to them, barking and going on. The lads were all over him, stroking him and patting him."

"What happened to him?" I asked. My fingers squeezed the headrest in front so hard that they ached.

"They must have had some food or something in a plastic bag one of them was carrying. Dog was jumping up at it, trying to get a sniff. It followed them across the park, and never came back."

I pushed my face into the back of the headrest until hot flashes of pain spread throughout my skull, and my brain felt as if it was being squeezed in a vice. If only I hadn't fallen asleep.

"After a while, when the dog didn't show up, I thought I'd go wake you up. I figured the dog was like a guide dog or something. But things got a little muddled in my head, and I remembered what your father said, not to let you guys know I was there. Find you, check you were all fine, then leave. I just kind of froze, until you took off. You're pretty fast for a blind kid, you know."

"Yeah, people say that."

"Scared the life out of me. I was worried you'd run right into a tree and break your damn neck. No way your father would've forgiven me for that one."

Dad laughed from the passenger seat.

"I still can't believe my blind son outran you. You need to

lose a few pounds, tubby."

"All right, I know. I could barely breathe by the time I caught him, then he was off again, after giving me a bruise the size of a teabag."

Oh, yeah – I'd kicked him good and proper, right in the shin. I sank down in my seat.

"Your leg, I'm sorry, I really didn't mean to kick you. I mean, I did, but I wouldn't have done it if I'd known you weren't trying to murder me."

"Dad," Pat said, breaking up my pathetic attempt at an apology. "Why didn't you come to see us when you found out where we lived?" His tone had hardened again. "Why did you send this guy instead?"

"I'm sorry, Pat. I've had some tough times lately. Lots of borrowed money that has to be paid back."

I had so much I was itching to know, but my body and my brain had submitted to exhaustion. Instead, I rested my head on the back of the seat and listened to the sounds outside that passed us by. Drills, horns, newspaper sellers screaming out the latest headlines. Such a far cry from the calls of the birds in the park that stretched around our home up north.

It almost came as a shock when the car pulled to a halt just a couple of minutes later and Leo announced that we'd arrived. I fumbled with my seatbelt, snapping it back across my chest, then I wrung my hands together and took a deep breath.

"Which one is it?" Pat asked, shuffling in his seat.

"Over here on the right, on the top floor. See the tulips in the window?"

"Oh. You like flowers, eh?"

"Well, it's not really my flat. The place belongs to my girlfriend, Alma."

"Your girlfriend? You have a girlfriend?"

"Yeah, why, is that so bad? Just because I'm your Dad, it doesn't mean I can't have a little fun, does it? Come on up and I'll introduce you."

We climbed out and Leo drove off, leaving us alone on the pavement – just me, Pat and Dad. Dad led us inside. When we reached the top floor – which was luckily just the first floor – Dad led us down a corridor and fished a set of keys from his pocket. He found the right one, then slipped it into the lock and jiggled it about until the door creaked open. Pat's hands appeared on my shoulders. He guided me gingerly forwards through the open doorway and a sudden rush of nerves had me trembling.

Here we were at last, inside Dad's home!

Unlike the rest of the building, the flat was soothingly warm. A lingering smell of burnt toast hung in the air, maybe only a few minutes old, mixed with the tang of spoilt milk. A recording of a woman's voice drifted from somewhere up ahead. She was muffled behind a door, but singing a slow, sad melody over the sound of a piano.

The door was suddenly pushed open, the bottom dragging against the thick carpet, and the words became clear.

"...*I never knew who you really were, concealed by a mask after all these years, now your face has slipped and your truth revealed, but my voice is gone, my attack unsteeled.*"

"Darrel?" called a different voice from the room beyond.

"Yeah, it's me!" Dad ruffled my hair again. "Come on, you two, no need to stand around in the hallway. Let's head through to the lounge, and I'll introduce you both."

He slid his arm across my shoulders and helped me down the corridor.

The CD was off now, and the only sound in the flat was the ominous ticking of a clock to my right, which sounded creepily similar to the Swiss clock back home.

"Hey there."

The words were spoken by a woman poised directly in front of me. I could already smell her perfume, a rich scent but somehow natural, like a forest after a downpour. Fresh and delicious.

"These are my two boys. This here is Joel." A squeeze of my shoulder, and I forced a smile and nodded politely. "And this is Pat."

"Hey."

"Boys, this is Alma. This is technically her flat, so be on your best behaviour."

"I'm his partner," Alma said, and I noticed her accent was foreign – almost certainly European, although which country, I had no idea. "Are you both okay? You look a little beaten up."

I touched a hand to my bandages.

"Oh, I just...banged my head falling over a couple of days ago. It's okay now. Just got a lump there, that's all."

"Who put the bandages on?" Dad asked.

I caught a snigger from Pat's direction, and my lips parted, but no words came out.

"It wasn't you, was it Pat?"

"Yeah, maybe."

"Why?" I asked, my stomach clenched. "What's wrong with them?"

"It's so cute," Alma said. She clapped her hands together. "Little teddy bears! So smiley!"

"Teddy bears? What teddy bears, what are you talking about?"

"Your bandages," Dad said, doing a pretty bad job of stifling a laugh. "They're covered in cartoon faces."

"Pat!" I curled my hands into fists and bared my teeth, but Pat was wise enough to step away, well out of range. I tore the bandages from my scalp, then unravelled the whole lot and stuffed them into my pocket.

"Anyway," Dad said, patting me on the shoulder. "Would anyone like a drink, or a snack?"

My stomach gurgled an instant reply.

"Can I have both?" I asked.

He chuckled. "No problem. Pat, you hungry too?"

"Yeah, food would be good, cheers."

Dad headed for the kitchen and myself and Pat took a seat beside Alma on a large leather sofa.

The leather was cold to the touch, and I carefully sank back into it, worried for a moment that I might disappear into some hidden crevice as the material morphed around my body.

"Good to finally meet you both," Alma said, shifting beside me.

Her voice was husky yet delicate, as if her throat would crack apart if she spoke any louder. "And it is a little strange, too. Darrel always told me what men you would become. I formed this picture in my head. Like Pat, I heard you loved to kick around an old football in the garden. We wondered if one day we'd watch England play and you'd be there on the pitch, scoring a goal." She let out a nervous chuckle, then cleared her throat. "You still like football?"

"Not really. Don't think I've played it since I was about four."

"Ah, that is a shame. What about you, Joel, you like to play sports?"

"He doesn't play sports," Pat said, placing a hand on my shoulder. "He's blind."

"I know he is blind. He can still live a normal life, though, right?"

I meshed my fingers and ground my knuckles against each other.

Pat paused for a moment before replying.

"So you hooked up with Dad, huh?"

There was a touch of menace in his tone, a kind of warning like a cat arching its back. I wished right then that the sofa really would swallow me up. The uncomfortable silence that followed was broken by a clattering of dishes from the kitchen, and a chain of curses from Dad.

"We have lived together for a couple of years now," Alma eventually replied, her tone cautious.

"You don't look very old. Not half as old as Mum."

"I'm nineteen."

"Nineteen? Bloody hell, I'm not too far off that! How come you want to go out with someone as old as Dad, then? He help you with your homework?"

My stomach collapsed with relief when Dad brushed his way through the door and handed us all plates stacked with food.

I balanced my plate on my knees and snapped open an ice-cold can that followed it. The contents turned out to be Fanta. The cool liquid cleansed my throat and I instantly felt normal again.

"Well, I really don't know where to begin," Dad said, sitting himself opposite us. "How is your Mum, really? Is she working again?"

"No, she ain't working."

My fingers traced over the food on my plate. Some kind of sandwiches cut into triangles, and a stack of crisps on the side. The sandwiches smelled like ham.

"What's wrong? Did something happen, back home?"

There was a terrible anxiety in Dad's voice. Something inside me stirred, and I desperately willed my brother to tell him what we had done.

My jaw clenched tight, but Pat remained silent.

"Pat, please, tell me. I need to – "

"She's dead." The words had left my lips before I'd even had a chance to think about them, as if some higher power had plied my vocal chords. Immediately my face flushed and my cheeks tingled. I stuffed a sandwich into mouth to stop any more words from emerging. Ham and cheese, with mayo. Not bad.

"She's what? Did you say she's dead?"

I chewed on the sandwich and wished I hadn't spoken.

Would it really have been that bad, not telling him? If we'd just pretended that Mum was alive and well, and she had a top job as some kind of manager or executive or whatever, and the reason we'd left home was simply to see more of the world, and she was perfectly happy with that? She could have even kissed us each on the cheek and handed us a packed lunch before waving us off, a hankie clutched in her hand to stem the flow of tears.

"Yeah," Pat said. "She's dead and cold."

"Well... God, I... How did it happen?"

"She fell, banged her head. Two days ago. She was drunk."

Dad sucked in one deep breath after another, until it sounded like he was hyperventilating.

I swallowed the lump of sandwich.

I didn't know whether to go over and hug him, or just sit right where I was and wait for something to happen. A confusing mixture of feelings suddenly burst forth, in a terrible eruption of emotion.

I was the one who'd lost Chops. I was the one who'd told Pat what had happened to my head. I was the one Mum had tried to grab when she slipped and fell. I was the one responsible for every terrible bloody thing that had happened.

Alma was the first to move. She slid off the sofa and I heard her embrace Dad. I knew I should do the same. It took all my concentration to push myself forwards, out of the deep depression in the sofa, without spilling any of the food. Eventually I managed it, and placed the plate by my feet. Cautiously I wrapped my arms around them both. Their hands crept over my back and clutched me.

"I can't believe it," Dad whispered. "So what happens now? When's her funeral?"

"Um..." Pat said, hesitating. "We don't know."

"You don't know when she's being buried?"

"Well, no. We haven't told anyone else."

"What do you mean?" I think it took a moment to register, but when he spoke again his tone had hardened. "You didn't call an ambulance when it happened? Or the police?"

"No."

Dad's fingers tensed, then his hand slipped from my back. Once again his breathing intensified. He rose from his seat and strode the length of the room, then he turned and headed straight back.

"Okay, then. What did you do with her? Is she still in the house, or did you just go ahead and bury her in the garden?"

"You're mad with us?"

"No, no... I'm not, I'm not mad. I'm just... This is a little too much to take in all in one go, you understand? It's like being hit by a car, and then falling right in the path of a train."

Right then, the doorbell rang.

I just stood there and listened to the endless ticking of the clock. Nobody moved or even spoke until the piercing buzz came a second time.

"Do you want for me to get it?" Alma asked.

Dad must have nodded, because she pulled away and strode past me and down the hall, towards the front door.

"Who is it?" she called.

"Detective Inspector Murphy, madam," came an exhausted-sounding voice from the other side of the door. "Looking for Mr Darrel Petersen."

The heavy breathing ceased and the entire room became still, as if time had ground to a halt.

"Darrel Petersen?" Alma called back.

"Do you know him?"

"Yes, I know him. Why, is something wrong?"

"Can you open the door please, madam?"

More silence. I wondered if Alma would refuse, but then I heard the lock rattle and the door creak open.

"There we go, much better. Do you know where we can find him?"

"No. I have not seen him for a few days. He just comes by sometimes, when he feels like it."

"And if I ask your neighbours if they've seen him recently, do you think they'd confirm that?"

"I'm sorry? You are saying I am a liar?"

"No, I just like to be sure, that's all. He's proving difficult to track down, and we're rather anxious to talk to him."

"What is this all about?"

"It's concerning his wife." The nausea returned like a punch to the belly. I could actually feel the blood drain from my face. "Can I just come in for a moment?" the detective asked.

"I would rather you didn't. I do not like having strange men in my apartment."

"Well, that's understandable. But we're in the process of obtaining a warrant, so you might as well just let us in now, eh? Save us all the embarrassment of forcing our way in?"

My entire body tensed, like a sprinter on the starting line waiting for the gunshot. A crash from somewhere downstairs almost startled me – the sound of raised voices, and a stampede of feet charging up to our floor. The voices grew in intensity, a mixture of furious bickering and random chatter. They drowned out the conversation between the detective and Alma.

"There he is," someone called out, their piercing tone cutting above all the others.

A jubilant cheer shot out from the hallway. The volume of it terrified me, but the invading gathering was cut off mid-roar by a terrific slam. Alma returned to the lounge.

"What the hell is going on?" Dad practically shouted to be heard over the chaos. He was still on his feet.

"There are three cops out there, wanting to speak with you," Alma said. "I told them you were not here, but they say they will get a warrant to come in. They found your wife's body. They are searching for Joel and Pat."

"What the hell are they getting a search warrant for, if all they want is to ask me some questions?"

"He said that they're treating the death as suspicious."

"Suspicious?"

"Maybe they think someone broke in," Alma said. "Killed your wife and kidnapped the boys."

Dad sighed, long and loud, as if he was deflating.

"I see. Someone like me, eh?" He cleared his throat.

"The lead cop, he said they've been putting out bulletins on the news all morning with pictures of the boys. Someone saw you with them earlier and reported it. Probably Mrs Harrison, big nose bitch, always squinting out through those horrible curtains."

"Oh, this is just perfect. What about all the others out there? It sounds like there's a bloody army invading."

"Pssh, journalists. A huge crowd of them followed the cop."

"What the hell for? Frigging parasites want an interview with me or something?"

"I did not stay to ask. We should probably draw the curtains, before someone else sees you."

Alma walked the circumference of the room and attended to each of the windows, while Dad cursed and muttered under his breath.

The voices were right outside the door now. Someone banged their fist against the other side, and a woman called for Alma to open up again.

"Miss Jasinski! Miss Jasinski, please, we only want a comment from you. Is it true you're romantically involved with Darrel Petersen? Did you know that his wife is dead, and his children are missing?"

More fists began to beat against the door. Now others called out, demanding that someone open up and speak with them.

"Well," Dad muttered, "we've got to talk to the police. Straighten this all out."

"No," Pat said, cutting Dad off. "No, wait. Don't do that."

"Why the hell not? Pat, can't you hear them all out there? They think your mother was murdered!"

"Yeah, well... Maybe it wasn't all an accident."

A beat of silence.

"What are you saying?"

"It wasn't your fault – " I started, but Pat talked right over me, shocking me into silence.

"I killed her. After she fell. She cracked her head good, knocked herself right out...but in a second she would've come round, right? And I just saw her lying there, and I didn't want her to get back up."

"Pat, what did you do?" Dad's voice crumbled, and I could almost hear his heart give up and collapse.

"I panicked." Pat's voice sank to a whisper. "I knew she was gonna get up in a minute and start screaming again. I had to keep her away from Joel. I just thought, she'll kill us both. I had to stop it right then. I could try to fight her off, but what about Joel? He was already in a mess." Tears ran down Pat's cheeks. "So – I grabbed the cushion from her chair and pushed it down over her face. I really pushed it hard. It was only for a few seconds, then I pulled it away, but then she looked dead for sure. So – I got into more of a panic and I tried to make her breathe again, but – "

The banging reached a crescendo. From outside the window there came the distant shrill scream of sirens, cutting down the street towards us. Dad let out a wail and lunged at Pat, and Alma shouted something, pleading with him. I cried out and stumbled forwards, my arms outstretched, just as the first of the police cars screeched to a halt outside.

Thirteen

Dad had his arms around Pat and clutched him tight, so tight that I couldn't tell whether he was crushing him or hugging him. I clung onto them both, unsure what to do until Alma's hands reached around my shoulders and plucked me away, giving me a squeeze.

"What had she done to you?" Dad asked, his voice hoarse. "What did she do to make you want to end it like that?"

"Just..." Pat started, his words sticking in his throat. "I didn't even think about it, I just panicked. It just happened. The way she was always screaming at Joel, I thought she'd kill him this time. I thought she'd kill us both."

They stayed like that, Pat gripped by Dad, for minutes.

Outside, the reporters were met by the roars of the police, who battled them away from the door. The banging finally ended, for now.

"What are we going to do?" I asked.

"We have to get out of here," Dad replied immediately. "I'm not letting those bastards get hold of either of you."

"But how we gonna get past the cops?" Pat asked.

"We can use the attic space. It's one long section that joins all the flats on this side of the corridor. Alma, grab the torch from the toolbox, and I'll get the ladders."

A minute later I was halfway up a set of stepladders. Dad's hands circled my wrists from above and helped me up into the attic. The ladders shook from side to side beneath my feet, despite Alma's efforts to keep them steady, and I thought they were going to collapse, leaving me kicking in mid-air.

When I was halfway in, Dad grunted and heaved me up.

The place was so cold, it was like being dragged into a giant freezer. The air was thick with dust which made my face itch and clogged my nostrils until I felt a sneezing fit coming. I crushed my nose between my fingers to quash it.

Pat had just started up the ladders when three violent thuds boomed out from the front door, and a gruff voice announced:

"Police, open up!"

Dad cursed then hissed down at Pat.

"Come on, son, hurry up!"

The police continued to pound on the door as Pat clambered up onto the beam beside me. They thumped it with such force that I was sure they would smash it down any second, and catch us in the middle of our escape.

The ladders scraped away beneath us.

"Miss Jasinski, this is your final warning! If you don't open up, we will have to break down the door!"

"Okay, okay!" she screamed back. "Let me put some clothes on! I will be there in a moment!"

The hatch was pushed back up and the lock clicked into place. Suddenly the shouting and the pounding seemed so distant, so unreal.

"We've got to be quiet," Dad whispered, his hand enclosing mine. "You both got that?" I nodded, my other hand still crushed over my nose. "Okay, follow me, but be careful. There's only thin planks of wood up here, and nothing but plaster between them. If you fall off, you'll go straight through someone's ceiling."

We started across the first beam just as footsteps charged into the flat below, our feet sliding sideways across the thin plank of wood. Dust billowed around my face and my skin itched even worse, the sensation spreading to my ears and right down the nape of my neck. I didn't dare take my hand from my nose, but all I could think about was raking my nails across the skin, scratching until it left me red and raw. I tried my best to put it from my mind, and instead concentrated on my feet. I shuffled along a few inches at a time as Dad guided me from the front, his hand still locked over mine. Pat was close behind.

We'd only moved a few paces when a tremendous crash from Alma's flat shook the beams below us. My left foot slipped from the wood and threw me off-balance. With a silent yelp I jerked to the side. My free hand shot from my nose and grasped at the mouldy air, desperately searching for a purchase, but my fingers clutched hopelessly at nothing. I felt myself tipping and I tensed my entire body, crushing Dad's fingers. Then another hand grabbed my sleeve and yanked me back towards the beam, while Dad's grip steadied me. In an instant I was back, two feet secure on the wooden strip.

"Careful, man," Pat whispered and he rubbed my shoulder. Even in my frantic state, I was surprised to realise that his touch was suddenly uncomfortable.

The thought was shot a second later. Now that my hand had been torn away, the dust cloud had infiltrated my nostrils. I held my breath as best I could and squeezed my nose once more with my free hand. Sneezing right now would end our chances for sure – that is, assuming no one had already heard us scrambling around.

Below, I could make out the voice of the policeman in charge as he barked out commands, allocating rooms for each of them to search. For now they had no idea we were right over their heads.

We worked our way across the beams at a painfully slow pace, occasionally clambering over the three-foot-high wooden divides that barely separated the attic spaces of each flat. Dad called back after the second divide, his voice still hushed.

"We're above an empty flat right now. If we can get down, we can hide in there."

"You want us to jump through the plaster?" Pat asked.

"No, bloody hell, don't do that! I'll see if I can open the hatch from up here. Both of you, crouch right down, as far as you can. If the police come into the attic, they won't see us over the divides."

We did as he asked and Dad crept away, in search of the hatch. The wait was horrific. For one, it was the first real chance I'd had to consider Pat's confession. The full horror of it crept down my spine and made me shiver. I'd stood by while he smothered her. I had been just feet away, too terrified to move, held rigid in the doorway of her bedroom. Did that make me an accomplice?

The penetrating silence was shattered by the sound of Dad grunting. Something heavy trembled across the beam we were squatting on, spreading itchy tremors through my hands and knees.

At that same moment, a sinister creaking echoed the length of the attic. Alma's voice drifted along behind it.

"You can't find anything up there. It's just cobwebs and dust."

"Madam, I won't warn you again, will you please step back!" That was a cop, the same one who'd been screaming outside the flat. The police were coming into the attic.

"Quick, come here," Dad hissed at us. I started in the direction of his voice. My hands stayed tight on the beam and I scraped my knees along the jagged wood. The sound of my jeans rubbing against the rough surface was unbearable, as jarring as a chainsaw motor in the quiet. I clenched my jaw and tried my best to lift my legs from the beam with each shuffle. However, doing so put me off balance and in danger of toppling off the beam, so I quickly abandoned the idea.

I was so focused on the scraping noise that it came as a shock when Dad's hand met mine on the beam. He slipped his fingers around my wrist and guided me to the hatch, which was hanging open.

"You're going to have to lower yourself down over the edge, then let go and drop to the floor. Understand?"

I nodded silently, hoping I somehow appeared brave to him even though my stomach lurched at the thought. The climb up to the attic was over twice my height. This was it though – the only means of escape. Back where we'd come from, the attic space creaked with the arrival of the searchers. Their voices were almost ghostly, a sinister chant that barely crept over a whisper. They were headed this way.

I swung my legs over the edge, then twisted my body around and gripped the wooden frame of the hatch. With steady urgency I eased myself downwards until the corner dug into my chest. My chin disappeared below and then I was simply dangling there, my hands still locked on the slab of wood above. I tried to stretch my toes out, even though I knew there'd be nothing beneath me. Sure enough, only air. With all my might I wanted to let go, but – but what if there was an endless chasm below, or a pit trap full of deadly spikes, like some barbaric burglar trap, ready to claim the life of anyone foolish enough to break in? I would be dead without even realising it.

For a few seconds I hung like a fish on a hook, until my arms screamed and my fingers finally relented. I plummeted, my stomach forced up my throat at the sudden motion, but for no more than a second. My ankles burned as I hit the ground and rolled over onto my side. The bare carpet did pretty much nothing to cushion my fall.

I was sprawled on my back and groaning pitifully when Pat hit the ground beside me. He staggered away but managed to stay on his feet. Dad followed straight after.

"Quick, Pat, help me with that chest of drawers."

The two of them slid the chest across the room, then Dad clambered on top and I heard the hatch click back into place.

"Crap, that was close," Pat said, his voice weary.

Dad sighed, and mumbled in agreement.

"We've got to be quiet, in case they search the attic space directly above. They can't come into this flat unless they've got just cause. You okay, Joel?"

"Fine," I whispered back. I sat cross-legged on the floor, massaging my ankle. Pat twitched next to me and rubbed his feet into the remains of the carpet.

"I thought this flat was empty? Still looks lived-in to me."

"It's empty for now. The old girl who owns the place just retired, so she's off on some round-the-world trip for a few months. We've just got to hope all her visas were valid. We're in trouble if she comes back early."

I'd already figured out that an old person lived here. I could tell from the smell of the place. Don't get me wrong, I've got nothing against old people – well, the nice ones at least – not the ones who barge past you and don't even say sorry. But they all smell quite distinct. It's not really a fusty or old smell – it's more of a mellow, ripe aroma, like a mature cheese or something. I've no idea why it happens. Maybe they all use the same type of washing powder, or something like that.

"How long do we have to stay here?" I asked.

"I don't know. Until it's safe for us to leave."

A sudden banging at the front door shocked us into silence. I felt another sickening turn in my stomach, like I was on some crazy rollercoaster.

"Police. Open up, please."

"Oh, frig," Pat whispered. "You think they know we're in here?" Dad was silent, so we stayed rigid and waited while another round of heavy knocks echoed around the flat. I held my breath for what seemed like at least ten minutes, but must have been no more than a handful of seconds. We heard people moving around outside, but no more knocks followed.

Eventually we relaxed enough to stretch our muscles and stagger from our statue-like poses. Dad sighed, then collapsed into a creaky chair.

The silence turned from anxious to uncomfortable, until Pat finally spoke up.

"I'm sorry I did it, if that counts for anything. But I wouldn't take it back. If I had the chance to do it over again, I'd smother her just the same. I'm glad she's dead."

He got no response, not for a while. When Dad did speak, his words were all choked up.

"Your own mother. She was really that terrible?"

"It was what I told you. She used to beat me, Dad. All the bloody time, for nothing at all. Then she started on Joel. See that gash?"

"She did that to him? His head?"

"Yeah, she did. Right, Joel?"

I nodded.

"If I'd known she could do something like that... I'm sorry, boys. I'm really sorry."

"What are you sorry for?" I asked, looking up. "You were searching for us all this time. You never gave up on us."

"I'm sorry for leaving in the first place, Joel."

"But you never had a choice, right? Mum kicked you out, didn't she?"

"She told you that?"

"Well, I…"

That was when I realised. We didn't actually know what had happened back then. We'd always just assumed that Mum had got rid of Dad, I guess because of the way she acted towards us – cold, all full of anger, like she'd be better off without us.

"You saying you just left us?" Pat said, his tone suddenly threatening.

"It all got messed up pretty bad," Dad said after a long, devastating pause. "I mean, things used to be great between your mother and me, back when we first met. We loved each other so much. Engaged after three months, married a month after that. That was when we were still at university. But then it all changed after we graduated, when she joined this law firm. I can't even remember the name any more.

"Soon she was head honcho, one of the main partners, and I barely ever saw her after that, even though we were still living together. She'd usually get in after I'd gone to bed, and be out again before I even woke up. Sometimes when she came back she'd sit out in the lounge for an hour or so, and I'd hear her crying to herself. If I got up to ask her what was wrong, she'd just say it had been a long day and she'd be fine in the morning. Wasn't long before I just stopped getting up.

"After a couple of years living like that, she came home early one day and told me she was pregnant. I couldn't have

157

been happier. I thought she would finally take some time off work and we could concentrate on raising a family together. Fresh start, I guess. And don't get me wrong, your mother was happy, too. But she seemed to take her pregnancy as some kind of challenge to be overcome, and she kept on pushing herself, working even harder than before. She was the first woman to ever be made a partner at the firm, and I guess this was her way of proving to all the men that she could still cope. It was just too much for her, she was a complete mess. As soon as you were born, and she was able to get around again, she went straight back to work. I stayed home, raising you by myself.

"I can't remember when it was, maybe a couple of months later, but I found a receipt in one of her coat pockets from this grubby little off-license down the street. That was when I found out she was an alcoholic. I showed her the receipt and she blew up, told me not to go searching through her stuff. She was hitting me and screaming in my face, and then she just broke down right in front of me, started crying and saying how sorry she was, how stupid she had been.

"We talked it over, and she told me how bad it was. Bottle of vodka every day, sometimes more. I was disgusted, but I really can't say I was surprised. We must have talked for hours, the first proper talk we'd had in months, and she seemed so much better after that. She promised she'd quit the booze and try and ease back at work a bit, spend some more time with us. And I believed her, like a total bloody idiot."

He paused and I heard him sob. I twisted my fingers together and ground my heels into the carpet and eventually he continued.

"For a year or so things were okay, or at least a little better than they had been. Your mother still worked ungodly hours, but she stayed off the drink and she seemed a lot more human in the fleeting moments we did spend together. Then she told me she was pregnant again, and again I was thrilled. I really thought that this was it. This would finally bring us back together. But your mother, she... she just lost control. She was convinced that falling pregnant again would cost her the job, that they'd replace her with a man instead, someone without a bloody womb. It was total crap, of course it was, but there was no reaching her.

"And then I caught her one morning, downing cheap vodka in the bathroom before she headed off to work. Straight from the goddamn bottle. She was already four months pregnant by then. It was exactly the same as before, like we'd just regressed an entire year. She was screaming at me, calling me these terrible things, then she stormed out of the flat.

"I don't think we spoke again for a couple of weeks, till she came home early one day, stinking of wine. The other partners had finally worked out what was going on and fired her. That really was the end. She would sit around the flat all day, just staring at the wall and occasionally breaking down into crying fits. I had to watch her all the time, make sure she didn't try to hurt herself. And that was when her mother, your grandmother, got involved.

"Her mother had been living over in the States for years, and I don't think she spoke to us once the whole time. Finally she decides to come back home, and the first thing she does is pay us a visit. Of course, when she sees how bad everything is, she naturally blames me for it all. And I guess in a way she was right. All that time I'd just sat back and watched your mother crumble away until there was nothing left. I could have stepped in at any time and got her help. Instead, I just waited and prayed that things would sort themselves out. That having kids would miraculously bring us back together. But there wasn't any hope for us. We were so broken that trying to fix us just made us worse.

"Your grandmother told me to leave, said she would take care of everything. Get out and don't come back, she told me. And I did just what she said. I went upstairs and found you sleeping, Pat, and I kissed you on your forehead and told you everything would be okay. Then I walked out of the house and didn't even turn back."

We'd sat there and listened to him speak, and now that he'd lapsed into silence I had no idea what to say. In truth, I didn't even know how to feel. Dad began to cry, huffing short raspy breaths and sniffing and snorting. I pushed my palms into my temples and wished that he would stop.

"Our grandmother must have left not long after you did," Pat said, breaking the uncomfortable silence. "I didn't even know she used to live with us. Mum told us her parents were both dead."

"You mean… Your mother raised you both herself?"

"If you can call it that. I took over raising Joel when I was old enough. Fed him, cleaned him, looked after him when he needed it. Why d'you even care, anyway? Why you so interested in us all of a sudden? Sending up that goon to spy on us when you were the one who walked out?"

"That's not fair," Dad said, his tone suddenly hard. "I never stopped thinking about you, not for a single bloody day. I tortured myself, wondering what would have happened if I'd stayed, if I could have made it work somehow. Right then, that moment I walked down the driveway and got into my car and drove away, I didn't think I had a choice. Now I know that I always had a choice, and I shafted it. I screwed up, Pat. I've had to live with that ever since."

"Well, your life sure sucks."

My lips curled at Pat's curt reply and I squeezed my palms together. Dad was heartbroken, I could tell. Even after his confession, even now that I knew he'd walked out on us all those years ago, before I was even born – I still wanted him to take us in and be part of our family again.

"I'm sorry, Pat. Both of you. I can't tell you how truly sorry I am. I just want to make amends, that's all."

"Yeah, whatever. Shame it took you so long, eh?"

"I tried in the past to get in touch, I swear to God. Not just through those stupid postcards, either. About eleven years ago I travelled up to the old house your mother and I bought just after we married, just in case you were still living there. Of course, you'd all left by then."

"And I guess you've never heard of Yellow Pages."

"Come on, Pat," I said. "Don't be so hard on him."

Pat just snorted. "You're taking his side?"

"I'm not taking anyone's side. I just don't want to argue. We came all this way to find him, remember?" I traced Dad's steps and found him slumped at one end of an old sofa. The wooden skeleton creaked ominously as I collapsed next to him, and Dad patted my leg.

"Please believe me when I say I tried everything I could think of to track you down," Dad said. "But I know I shouldn't have waited so long. I'll make it up to you both, I promise."

Pat had no reply, for a change. I was too relieved for words, and too exhausted to do any more than collapse against Dad. My limbs felt like plasticine snakes that dangled uselessly from my body. I rested my head against his shoulder, bony but comforting through the thin material of his T-shirt. Soon the voices from the corridor had been reduced to a dull rumble, and I slipped into exhausted sleep.

Fourteen

When I woke up, Dad was no longer beside me. I was splayed out on the sofa with an old cushion stuffed under my head. The smell of the worn fabric alone was enough to make me sit up and perch on the edge. Apparently a cat – or perhaps several – had once used the cushion as a bed, or worse.

At first I was confused, a bit startled, but then the moment of amnesiac bliss crumbled away, and everything that had happened came rushing back. I let out a deep groan. I squeezed the nape of my neck to massage some life back into the muscle, then called out to Dad and Pat. There was no response, but a few seconds later I heard something clatter to the ground in the distance, followed by mumbled curses. The sounds came from another room, off to the left.

I staggered to my feet and stretched. A pause while my head cleared, then I made in the direction of the noise. My arms were spread out in front of me as I didn't know this flat at all. After just a few steps, it showed. The side of my knee smacked into the edge of a table, and I silently screamed and clutched at the bone. I tried my best not to crash into more furniture as I hopped around in a frenzy, my tongue clamped between my teeth.

It took a while for the flashes of pain to subside. When they finally did, I hobbled away from the table, this time edging sideways so any other sharp corners would catch the fleshy part of my leg instead of the bone. My fingertips finally found a wall and I followed it until I came across a closed door. Behind the door I could hear a faint rustling and hushed portions of a conversation. I couldn't make out the words, but it was clearly Dad and Pat. My fingers slid along the edge of the door until they bumped into the smooth, cold metal doorknob. A quick twist and the door drifted open.

"Oh, hey," Dad said, his voice hushed and a little croaky. "You're up. You sleep okay?"

"Not bad," I said, although in all honesty I felt even rougher than before – like I'd spent the last two days tied to the back end of a rhino. "What time is it?"

"Just gone four in the afternoon. The corridor gathering's disappeared, but Alma texted an hour ago to say there's a couple of guys still hanging around outside. We better stay here till they've headed off too, then we can make a move. Anyway, come on in, join us. Pat and me were just searching around for some food."

Pat sighed, a clear sign that the search had proved unsuccessful.

"There's nothing in here but cat food and gravy." He tossed some tins on the floor and they scattered across the room, rolling over the cold floor tiles. "Gonna make a tasty meal, huh?"

"Hey, remember this isn't our flat. Try not to wreck it."

"The old bag that lives here must be nuts. How could anyone live off this stuff?"

I shuffled my way into the kitchen and found a counter to lean against, accidentally kicking aside a can in the process. The air between Pat and Dad was still tense, but I chose to ignore it for now. Instead, I focused on the itchy dryness at the back of my throat.

"Do we have anything to drink?"

"Sure," Pat replied. "Do you like gravy?"

"There's a tap over here, Joel. I'll get you a glass of water. Just ignore your brother, he's cranky as hell."

For hours we sat around in the empty flat. The hungrier we got, the more Dad and Pat griped at each other. Eventually though, Pat wandered off to the bedroom, and I had a chance to finally talk with Dad.

He told me all about his life, all the stuff I was dying to know. His childhood, and the grandparents I had never met, who had both died in a car wreck long before I was born.

He told me about London and the parts of it that he loved to visit. His favourite was a small corner of Hyde Park, where he could sit underneath a great Oak and feed the birds.

"My first flat was just on the edge of the park. Not a flat really, more of a tiny room. Had a fold-down bed and a sink and not much else, except rot and rats."

"Sounds pretty bad."

"Yeah, but it was all I could afford. Now I've got a bigger place up the street, but I spend a lot of time here with Alma."

"So…"

I paused as I wondered how to tactfully word my next question.

"So…what?"

"I was just wondering about you and Alma."

"Oh? What about us?"

"Are you two really... boyfriend and girlfriend?"

I pulled a face the moment the words left my lips. I was desperate to know, but the question sounded so dorky.

Dad gave a quiet little laugh and patted me on my knee, the one I had cracked off the table just a short while before, which made me wince further.

"Yeah, we have been dating. She's a really sweet girl, got a huge heart. Came over to the country a year ago, from Poland. I was the first British person she spoke to. She's been following me around ever since."

"She seems nice."

"Yeah, she is. I know you and Pat will get on great with her."

I wasn't so sure about Pat, but I didn't say anything to Dad. Instead, I tried to work out how to change the subject to something else important – what Dad actually did for a living.

Unfortunately, I only managed to get two words out before I was cut off by a timid rapping at the front door. Dad immediately tensed. He held still for a moment, then eased himself as stealthily as possible from the sofa.

"Stay here," he whispered. He crept across the room to the door. Another quick succession of raps came from the other side and this time a voice called out.

"Hey, it's Leo. Open up, there's no one about."

"Leo, thank God."

The chain lock clattered loose and Dad yanked the door open. Leo dragged himself into the flat and collapsed next to me with a satisfied grunt, mumbling hello while adjusting himself. Every awkward movement caused the rickety old sofa to cry out in agony, and I was sure the entire frame would collapse any second, taking both of us with it. The fact it had even survived his landing was nothing short of a miracle.

"So, how's it look out there?" Dad asked. He secured the door then strode back to the centre of the room.

Leo sighed and shuffled once more, and I caught a whiff of his aftershave – the same toxic fragrance he'd been wearing that day in the park.

"Cops have a couple of plain-clothes guys posted in a car right outside, keeping tabs on the block. Got out and stopped me, asked me who I was, soon as I tried getting in. Said I was just a friend of Alma's. Thought they were going to pull their truncheons and beat me to a pulp when I said her name. Made me show my ID."

"Did they escort you up or anything?"

"Nah, nah. One of them was straight on his radio, phoning me in. Just checking up I guess. Let me past as soon as they got the all-clear."

"Looks like we're stuck here for a little while longer, then. We can't jump out the windows on this side, they'll spot us easy." Dad began to pace again and occasionally made sharp clicking noises with his tongue. Eventually, he stomped to a halt and snapped his fingers. "What's Michael up to this evening?"

"Michael? Back home as usual. Probably playing Xbox."

"I'll give him a call." Dad walked up to the sofa. He crouched before me and patted me on the knee – the uninjured one this time. "Joel, could you go speak to Pat for me? Just explain that he's got to be ready to make a move in about twenty minutes. We're getting out of here, okay?"

"Okay." I pushed myself from the sofa, then Dad helped me across to the bedroom where Pat had barricaded himself. I nudged the door open and slipped inside, closing it softly behind me.

The room was, to quote an old horror tale, as silent as the grave. A bitter rosemary smell lingered in the flat, tepid air. The sickly scent would probably cover the reek of rotting flesh quite well. I hugged myself and rubbed at my forearms, where the skin had already begun to goosepimple.

"Pat? Hey, you awake?"

"I heard what he said already." From his fierce tone I could tell my brother was annoyed, like a child who's just been scolded. "He's come up with some brilliant plan, right? We'll probably end up crawling through some bloody sewers this time."

"Lay off, Pat. He's just trying to help us."

"I can't believe you're still defending him! Didn't ya hear him before? He just buggered off and left us! I knew coming here was dumb."

I didn't feel like pointing out the whole trip had been his idea.

"Can't you just forgive him? We haven't got anyone else, he's our only family now."

"We've got each other. Us two. Why do we even need anyone else? Screw 'em all."

I made my way across the room and found Pat sprawled on the edge of a tall bed. I squirmed up onto the mattress, which barely gave at all under my weight, then I clasped my hands together and ground my knuckles hard.

"D'you think I did the right thing?" Pat asked.

"What do you mean?"

"You know what I mean. You know how she was, how she'd beat the crap out of me for nothing. I didn't really care, as long as she left you alone, but look what she did. When she tripped on the frigging carpet, it just seemed so perfect, like right then there really was a God, and he stopped Mum before she could do anything else to us. Some proper fire and brimstone crap. When she was lying there with blood seeping outta her head, I thought for sure she was dead. I thought we were free. But then I saw her lips move, and all that relief just

168

went..."

He shuddered and sucked in a sharp breath. For a moment I thought he would collapse into tears right there before me. My knuckles throbbed as I unclenched my hands and grabbed a chunk of duvet, then rocked back and forth on the edge of the bed. I wondered whether I should say something, but before I could open my mouth, he started again.

"I didn't think anyone would find out. I thought they'd reckon she died from the fall. Crap, I really killed her, eh?" More nervous laughter – just as I'd heard back in Mother's bedroom, after the deed had been done.

I shook my head. "It's okay. We've just got to listen to Dad. He'll get us out of here." My tone was so flat that I couldn't even convince myself.

"Where we running to? Where we gonna hide?"

His question caught me off-guard. I had no idea where we could go to escape, where we could go to start our new life together. "I don't wanna leave here. I wanna just stay." His tone had changed again. Now he was almost pleading, and he slid across the bed and grabbed my arm. His fingers dug into my wrist and pulled me close. Pinpricks of spit rained onto my cheek, then were swept away by a hot gust from his nostrils.

"Tell him, Joel. Tell him we should just stay here, yeah?"

"We can't." I squirmed in his grasp and he let me go, but then his arms flew around me and his face plunged into my neck, leaving a smear of fresh wetness across my skin.

"Please, Joel. Please." He just kept repeating those words over and over.

I couldn't bear it. Nothing inside of me could ever accept what he had done, but my heart pounded so hard I could barely breathe, and I hugged him back until he fell into silence. His tears gradually dried, becoming sticky streaks on my neck.

"We'll be okay. Dad's going to make everything okay."

Finally he nodded, then sniffed and rolled off the bed.

"C'mon, then."

Dad was stood by the window when we emerged from the bedroom. Pat and I joined his side and waited in silent expectation, until he patted me on the back.

"Good timing," he said. "We'll be heading out in about five minutes. Leo's gone to warn Alma."

"How are we going to get past the police?" I asked as I leaned against the windowsill.

The constant drone of traffic from earlier was gone, the street outside now calm and silent. Dad had drawn back the curtains just an inch, so there was a large enough gap for him to see out, but not enough for people outside to look in.

"I've organised a distraction, should be arriving soon. As soon as those bastards outside move, we've got to leg it out of here and head straight for Leo's car. It's parked just to the right once we get out the front door. Think you two can manage that?"

"Sure," I replied, but Pat remained silent. "Um, Dad?"

"Yeah, Joel?"

"Where are we actually going? I mean, once we get out of the flat?"

"We're getting out of this bloody country. Somewhere the cops aren't going to find us. Then we can start all over again, like a proper family."

"We're going abroad?" The very idea shook me. I'd never even been this far from home in all my life, and now we were leaving England entirely?

"But, how are we going to leave? We don't have passports,

or..."

"Passports won't be necessary. I can get us a boat."

"A boat?"

"Yeah, I know one that's moored up at Ramsgate. That'll get us where we want to go."

I didn't know what to say. I just stood there and contemplated the fact that if we somehow evaded the massive police manhunt, and avoided a lifetime of prison, I would likely spend the rest of my life in exile in some foreign land. That was quite a lot to absorb on a Monday evening.

The distraction, as Dad called it, eventually pulled up on a back-firing moped.

"Here we go," Dad whispered, his voice an octave higher. "This is the guy."

"What guy?" Pat asked. He nudged me aside to peer through the curtains.

"Our saviour. He's going to run interference with the sentries. As soon as they're all off down the street, we get the hell out of here. Just have to pray that both of them give chase, or we're stuffed."

I held my breath and waited with tensed muscles for the sign that we had to move. It came with a tremendous roar from just outside the window, then several obscenities followed by a series of barked commands to 'stop right there', which I half-expected to be accompanied by a flurry of whistle-blows and sirens. Instead, the screams and shouts merely faded into nothing.

Just before they were out of earshot, Dad grabbed hold of my shoulder.

"That's it, go!"

We burst out into the hall and met up with Leo and Alma,

who were stood by the stairs. They greeted us with a hurried grunt. Seconds later we flooded outside, out where the traffic buzzed and the distant sirens wailed. My reflex reaction was to turn away, but Dad kept his hands clamped to my shoulders and forced me towards Leo's car. As soon as we got there, he yanked open one of the rear doors and shoved me inside with so much force that I almost face-planted the floor rug. I was then crushed against the door as Alma squeezed in next to me, followed by Pat, both cursing and muttering to themselves.

Leo and Dad climbed in the front, their doors slamming in perfect unison.

"Come on," Dad screamed, "start this heap of crap!"

"Trying to find the key," Leo shouted back, amidst a jangle of metal. "Turn the light on, will you?"

"You've got to be bloody kidding! You didn't think to find it before?"

"Stop shouting, you're making me nervous!"

"Oh well, I'm sorry, I hope I didn't hurt your feelings! Get a frigging move on!"

"Hang on, hang on..."

The engine squealed and then exploded into a furious fit of revs, and I was thrown back into the seat by a sudden burst of acceleration. In my right hand I clutched at my seatbelt, but the buckle was somewhere underneath Alma, out of reach. I didn't even realise at the time, but my left hand was wrapped tight around her arm.

"Crap," Dad said, barely audible over the protests of the engine. "There he is. They've got him down on the ground. Come on, drive, for God's sakes! They've spotted us!"

"Don't worry about it. Never going to catch us now anyway, even if they figure out they've been had."

"Just stick to the back roads, I don't want to take any chances."

We swung around a couple of bends, then Leo eased back a little. My stomach finally unclenched. I wriggled in my seat, trying to make the most of the little space I had. The car interior was chilly, but Alma's body, pressed against mine, was warm and comforting. I let her warmth seep onto me.

"Who was he," Pat asked. "The guy who distracted 'em?"

"That was Michael, my stepson," Leo said, with a hint of pride. "Does what he's told, bless him."

"Aren't you bothered he got nicked?"

"He's a smart lad, that one. Can talk his way out of a war. I bet in half an hour, he's having a pint with the coppers down the local." Leo chuckled to himself and drummed his fingers on the steering wheel.

"Be sure to thank him for us," Dad said.

"No problem. Bit of the radio?"

"Go for it."

The chorus of 'I wish it could be Christmas every day' kicked into life through a speaker just above my head. I shuddered and leaned away, my head crushed between my hands. I really couldn't stand that song – or Christmas songs in general, to be honest. Half of them are miserable, about people breaking up or being alone or whatever, and the other half are far too cheery. I always wished they would do something in-between, a kind of 'Christmas is okay, isn't it,' song.

Anyway, it was the final chorus, and the late-night DJ's caffeine-buoyed tones soon drowned out the awfulness of the music.

He blabbered on for a minute or so about how rubbish the postal service is this time of year, then his rant was cut off by a short jingle and a booming introduction to the hourly news update.

"Turn it up," Dad said, and Leo did so. The news reporter briskly announced that it was eleven pm, then immediately launched into a story that made the hairs on my arms stand on end, despite being buried in my jacket sleeves.

"Police are investigating the death of a forty-five-year-old woman in New Malsdone, North Humberside. Irene Petersen's body was discovered late last night after neighbours reported a disturbance. Mrs Petersen's two sons, aged twelve and fourteen, are currently missing, although witnesses claim to have spotted them with their father in South West London earlier today. Police are appealing for information – "

"Enough of that," Dad said, and the radio was flicked to another station. My face sagged and a tired squeak of disappointment eased from my lips – 'I Wish It Could Be Christmas Every Day' was only just beginning. With a troubled frown, I sank (or rather, wriggled) my way into the seat and sighed. Something was bugging me, and it wasn't just the awfulness of the music.

"Hey, Pat?"

"Yeah?"

"What do you think they meant by a disturbance?"

"Huh?"

"On the radio, they said our neighbours reported a disturbance."

"Oh. I don't know, didn't even think about it. Seems kind of odd, eh?"

"Maybe it could have been Chops?"

"Chops?" A pause, and he groaned. "Oh, man, maybe you're right. Would be typical of that dumb dog to find his way back and give us up like that. Probably barked his head off outside the door till that old biddy beside us went round to shut him up."

"Yeah, that's probably it, right?" I smiled and squeezed my legs together.

After a while the warm, fuzzy feeling in my gut was replaced by an inexplicable numbness. The music was making my head ache, so I asked Dad to change the station.

"You don't like Christmas songs?" Alma asked as a strange old country and western tune took over.

"Not really."

"What kind of music do you like?"

"I don't know. I guess I like some rock stuff."

"I like rock too. Have you heard of Decapitated?"

"Mmm, noooo, I don't think so. Are they from Poland?"

"Yes. They are *so* good for releasing your anger. If someone pisses you off, you can just listen to their album, I Hate Your Face and I'd Like You To Die, and scream and yell, and get over it. Your Dad does not like them much, he says they are too shouty. He prefers REM and Bruce Springsteen. They are not as good for releasing your anger." I must have looked completely confused, because then she said, "Come on. Who is your favourite group?"

"I kind of like Green Day."

"Ah, yes, the punk Americans. I suppose they are okay. Nothing like Decapitated though. Decapitated could have them all for breakfast."

A grin stretched my lips and it felt good, like it was the first time I'd smiled in months.

"Ahh, there you go. A happy look at last. You have a beautiful smile, Joel. You should use it more often."

I lowered my head, my cheeks burning hot. Her velvety fingers slipped under my chin and lifted my face again, turning me towards her. "Don't be shy." Her voice was more soothing than the hug of a big, warm duvet, and I couldn't help but beam further, flashing her a glimpse of my teeth. "There, keep it that way, okay? What about you, Pat? Do you like Green Day?"

"Nah," he replied in a slow and distant haze, as if his mind was in a different plane of reality. "It's just noise."

"Not a fan of rock music? What kind do you prefer?"

"Trance, house. Bit of hardcore sometimes."

I bit my lip and tried my absolute hardest not to add, *"and, of course, Rick Astley."*

"Club music? You're not a bit young for that?"

"You're one to talk."

"I don't like clubbing, anyway," Alma said, a hint of stress in her tone. "Too many sweaty bodies forced into one tiny space. Everyone drunk or out of it on drugs, yuck. Not for me. I prefer a hot soapy bath with some candles that smell nice. You know, the herbal ones."

Interesting mix, I thought. Heavy metal bands and scented candles.

"Have you heard of Bob Marley?" I asked her.

"Bob Marley? Of course! You like him?"

"I met someone who does. She told me a joke about him."

"What is the joke?"

"Well, she never actually told me the punch line. She forgot."

"Was it the one about doughnuts?" Pat asked. I turned to him and nodded.

"Yeah, that's it! Have you heard it?"

"Course, who hasn't?"

"What is the joke?" Alma asked again.

"How does Bob Marley like his doughnuts?" Pat paused for a beat, then answered: "With jam in."

The punch line was met with a sceptical "Oh." I mulled it over, but it didn't make any sense to me.

For the next ten minutes Dad guided Leo through various backstreets, before telling him to pull over. The car shook to a sudden halt and almost threw me into the back of the driver's seat.

"Why we stopping already?" Pat asked.

"Just hold tight," was Dad's reply. The leather seat cover let out a squeaky fart as he twisted around. "I've got to sort out one last thing before we head to the coast. I'll be right back, okay?" Both front doors creaked open and the car shook once more. The dashboard gave off a kind of low-pitched warning noise, then the doors slammed shut again and the noise died. Two sets of footsteps disappeared across the empty streets.

"Hang on," Pat said. "I recognise that building down there. The big 'un with the arch in the middle. We're right next to that frigging pub!"

"What pub?"

"Davey's bloody pub! The Prince Regent!"

"What? Are you sure?" I squeezed my knees tight and dug my nails into my skin. "Alma, why did Dad stop here?"

"I do not know, Joel." She pushed her arm across my shoulders and hugged me tight. "Let's wait, like he said." I nodded and rested my head against her chest. Her fingers swept through my hair to massage my scalp.

The previously-silent streets were coming alive now. Distant sirens screamed over the short, sharp, peppered explosions of fireworks and what sounded like some kind of wolf-like creature, which howled passionately into the night. Another car rolled up from behind and I shrank down in my seat, afraid that it might be the police, but it continued past us unannounced.

Its soft purr faded down the street, in the same direction Dad and Leo had disappeared.

"This is torture," Pat said. "What the hell are they doing?"

"Why don't we talk about something to keep our mind off it?" I suggested, my hand clasped to my knee to stop my entire leg from jiggling.

"Like what?"

"I don't know. Maybe Alma could tell us why she left Poland and came over here?"

"You really want to know?" she asked, her fingers entwined in my hair.

"Yeah. Didn't you like it over there?"

"Oh, I loved it. But I had to leave, sadly, because I murdered a young boy." I swore I felt my blood freeze within my veins, the moment she rested her nails on my scalp.

"You...killed someone?"

"He was probably about your age. About your height also. He even had the same colour hair..."

She tugged on a strand at the front of my head and I yelped and practically leapt through the roof of the car. Pat burst into uncontrollable laughter, even when I landed in his lap and clawed at his clothes. Then I realised Alma was laughing too. My cheeks were aflame.

"You were lying!"

"Just a joke," Alma said, and she pulled me back and hugged me tight. "Of course I have never killed anyone. I only left Poland because there was nothing there for me." Her laughter faded, and she coughed into her fist. "I did not have any family ties, no job, not much of anything. I just knew it was time."

Ahead of us, the fireworks died as abruptly as they'd started, but sirens continued to echo all around us, now closer than before. Pat's mirth at my gullibility was shattered by a sudden agitation.

"Where the hell are they? I can't believe they just left us sitting in the frigging car like this! The frigging cops are coming!"

"Calm down," Alma said, her voice as calm and soothing as ever. "We will be safe in here."

"Like frig we will," Pat shot back. He was so frantic that I honestly thought he would barge his way out of the car and sprint off. Maybe he would have done, but somewhere up ahead a set of tyres screeched, followed by the clatter of something hard and hollow being smashed across the street. A car blasted straight down the road towards us, or something bigger – a van, maybe. From the terrifying noise, it was clearly set on destroying everything in its path.

Fifteen

The van shot towards us at an incredible speed. The hideous roar of the engine built to a shocking crescendo, until I was certain it would smash straight into us and send us hurtling across the road.

"What is it? Who's coming?" I shouted over the noise. My hands clutched at Alma's leg.

"I... I cannot see, the headlights are blinding me." She pulled me close. I could feel her heartbeat against my skin and I heard her breath catch in her chest. I braced myself.

But there was no collision, no wrenching of metal, as the van skidded to a standstill right beside us. I already knew it was the cops. Dad's dream for us to flee the country and live in some exotic foreign land was about to end just ten minutes from his flat. A whimper of frustration escaped my lips, but Pat shouted over me.

"Holy crap, it's Dad!"

In a beat Pat was outside. The icy air whipped in through the open door, then Alma pushed her way out with me in tow. I could hear Dad's voice now. He was sitting inside the van, shouting at us to hurry up. Was this the reason he had stopped here, just to change cars?

My head buzzed as I was bundled into the back of the van, again almost ending up in a belly-flop on the floor. Pat was already inside, and he helped me up as Alma slammed the doors closed. Dad wasted no time in pulling away. The tyres screeched again the very moment Alma climbed up front. Even with the doors closed, the sirens outside screamed so loud that my eardrums buzzed deep in my skull. They appeared to be surrounding us. I was almost glad that I couldn't see outside, as my previous meal of sandwiches and crisps was already halfway up my throat, ready to explode across the inside of the van.

"Where's Leo?" Alma asked, and that was the first I knew that the fat man was not in the van with us. Before Dad could answer we jerked around a corner at full speed, the force so great that the two right wheels lifted clear off the ground for a full second before they slapped back down onto the broken tarmac with a wail of grinding metal parts. Pat tumbled on top of me and we crashed to the floor. Dad grunted from the driver's seat, cursing to himself.

"I lost him."

"Lost Leo?" Alma repeated, her voice raised. "You mean…?"

"We got separated. Cops were everywhere. But I got the boat keys in my pocket."

We ploughed around another bend, and this time I was the one who sprawled across Pat. Spasms of pain shot from the base of my spine as we crunched over a pothole.

"Here, back this way," Pat said, and he tugged at my jacket. "There's some sacks we can lie on." He half-dragged me towards the front of the van and deposited me on a soft pile, then collapsed beside me.

Lying amongst the sacks was a glorious relief after being crushed in the back seat of the car. Not quite as comforting as a soft mattress, but a definite improvement. I closed my eyes and stretched out my limbs, then let out a satisfied groan.

Even though my body cried out for rest, my brain was still annoyingly active, replaying every last surreal scene from the movie my life had become. It was pretty apparent by now that

Dad wasn't just some ordinary guy. I even suspected this wasn't the first time he'd been on the run from the cops, as he seemed to be handling it like most people would deal with a flat tyre. Nothing more than a minor inconvenience, get over it and get on with your day.

I wondered if he was some sort of criminal mastermind, well used to all these death-defying chases and last-minute escapes. A dirty mobster, along with Davey and all those other goons we'd met in the basement of the Prince Regent.

But could Dad really be such a person? He seemed so *nice*. After all, he liked to sit in Hyde Park and feed the birds, and he'd even made us ham and cheese sandwiches, with lots of mayo.

Then a terrible thought flashed through my mind – Dad throwing chunks of bread laced with poison to a gaggle of unsuspecting geese, and then dancing an evil jig around their corpses as they flapped and spluttered their last. Then an even worse thought – him slipping poison into a ham and cheese sandwich, and covering the bitter taste with lashings of mayo. I clutched my throat and ground my teeth, but managed to shake the idea with a shiver. Dad was most definitely not like that. I felt I was a fairly good judge of character, and I couldn't imagine our father hurting anyone or anything…at least, not without provocation.

So then I came up with the second theory, one which I admittedly stole from a book I'd once read. The book was about an undercover cop who infiltrated a drugs operation to 'bring it down from within'. He does all these horrible things which make him sick, to try and gain the trust of the criminals. He's even forced to kill one of his friends to prove that he isn't a cop, something which he cries about night after night (because he's sensitive and stuff). In the end he busts the crime lord and finally returns to his family, but he's changed so much that they don't even recognise him any more. It's like he already died inside, and now he's just a ghost that wanders the Earth, alone and miserable. Perhaps that was Dad's fate – he had infiltrated Davey's gang for the greater good, and was now a conflicted mess of a man.

My thoughts were shredded by a siren blast somewhere to my right. The piercing screech closed in on us. I held my breath, but the siren passed right on by and disappeared as quickly as it had appeared.

"That was close," Alma said, and she released a powerful breath.

"Telling me," Dad said. "Keep an eye out, let me know if you see any more flashing lights."

But there were no more lights and no more sirens. Not even any other cars as far as I could tell. We just kept on driving, headed further east until Dad announced that we'd left London. The tension lifted a little at last. Pat had even started to doze off beside me. Our whispered conversation about nothing at all grew more sporadic, and finished when Pat's only response was a long, loud snoring drone. I linked my hands behind my head and hummed a quiet tune, wondering to myself how all of this would end.

Part Four... How it ends

Sixteen

Alma eventually dozed off, just like Pat. Their snoring was almost perfectly synchronised so that just as one finished, the other began. Dad must have noticed this too, and he chuckled and sighed to himself from the driver's seat.

"How you doing back there, kiddo?" he asked, his voice soft so he didn't wake the sleeping pair. Knowing Pat, I think it would've taken a lot more than us talking to wake him – perhaps a pneumatic drill tearing a hole in the roof would have caused him to stir a little.

"Not too bad, thanks. Wish I could sleep as easy as Pat."

"Yeah. Hope it's not too uncomfortable back there. Afraid that this was the best I could do at such short notice."

"It's fine," I said with a smile.

"Oh, and by the way – happy Christmas."

"Christmas?" I hadn't even realised, with the crazy happenings of the last few days. It was past midnight, which meant it was Christmas Day. "Yeah! Merry Christmas, Dad!"

"Promise I'll get you a present as soon as I get a chance. The biggest, bestest present ever."

"Don't worry about it, really." I rubbed the back of my neck, which ached with tension. "I'm just sorry you're having to go through all this because of us."

"Don't ever bloody apologise, Joel." He tapped his fingers against the steering wheel and sighed. "Ever since I left, I wished we could come together again like this. Then when it finally happens, we end up on the lam in some busted-up van. Why does everything always turn out so bloody crazy?"

"I'm not sorry things turned out this way."

"You're not?" He sounded more than a little shocked.

"Nope. All we wanted was to find you, and now we have. Besides, it's been kind of fun."

"Fun?" Suddenly he was in fits of raucous laughter, coughing and choking between each burst of hysterics. I dug my heels into the pile of sacks and grabbed folds of the rough material as tight as I could, terrified that we'd veer from the road and plough into a ditch. Dad somehow managed to keep control, although his laughing fit stirred Alma from her sleep.

"What is it? What happened?"

"Ah, nothing, babe. Sorry to wake you." His laughter declined to a chuckle.

The two of them started a hushed conversation, so I lay back and stretched out again. My hand fell to my side, and immediately I winced and pulled it away. My knuckles had caught something hard, half-buried beneath the sacks. I dug in the material until I'd uncovered some kind of metal box, the surface grimy and covered in dents. The lid was held in place by two catches, but I flicked them up and the whole top half of the box lifted off.

"Buried treasure?" I whispered to myself. My fingertips delved inside and found a bumpy, cold chunk of metal. I pawed at it, unsure what it was. Eventually I pulled it out and held it carefully in my palm. The thing was heavy, and a sort of skewed L-shape. One end was quite smooth, while the other was reinforced with some kind of grip. I held it by the grip and noticed there was another chunk of metal that jutted out by my index finger.

When I realised what it was, my jaw dropped and my hand began to shake.

"Dad! Dad!"

"What? What is it?"

"I found a gun!"

"You what?"

The van swerved to the left and I almost tumbled off the pile of sacks, the gun still clutched tight in my fist. Pat was less fortunate. I heard a dull *thunk*, followed by a surprised yell.

"Arrghhh! What the bloody hell!"

He scrambled around at my side while Dad steered the van straight again. Both Dad and Alma screamed back at me from the cabin, but I couldn't hear them over each other. I was terrified to move my hands or lay the gun down, but I was shaking so hard that I thought I might drop it or somehow fire it by accident.

"What do I do?" I yelled. At my side, Pat picked himself up with a grunt.

"My sodding head, I bashed it right off the side of... woah, what the hell are you doing with that? Jesus, put it down!"

"What if it goes off?" I was near hysterics.

"Just stop waving it about! Argh, don't point it at me! Dad! Dad!"

"Joel, just relax, okay," Dad yelled from the front, but having him scream at me didn't help me to relax at all. "Pat, just take it from him and be careful! Don't touch the trigger!"

"Bollocks to that," Pat yelled back, "I'm not going anywhere near him!"

"Come on, you can do it."

I held as rigid as possible, and felt Pat's fingers enclosed mine. He had to practically wrestle the gun from me, but finally he prised it free. I gasped and slumped back into the sacks while Pat handed it to Dad.

"Okay, you did good. Where did you find this, Joel?"

"It was in a box, under the sacks."

"Pat, check there's nothing else in there."

"I really thought you were going to shoot me," Pat muttered as he searched the box. I was still in a daze. "Not much else, just some bullets and some papers."

"Okay, pass it up here."

The box was shifted into the driver's cabin. Pat slumped down at my side and let out a nervous chuckle.

"That was pretty intense, huh?"

"I'm just going to lie still," I said, my voice unnaturally high. "Just lie still and breathe and that's it."

"Uh oh," Alma said from up front, and I held my breath and waited for the next fantastic piece of news. "I can see lights behind us."

"Police?" Dad asked.

"In the sky. It looks like a helicopter."

"Damn it, that's all we need. Yeah, that's a copter all right. Searching the bloody road."

"You think they are looking for us?"

"Wouldn't surprise me. They must've figured out we're in this van by now."

"What we gonna do?" Pat asked. His voice trembled, and I felt him tense up beside me.

"Get off the road. There's a cut-off just up ahead." A few seconds later, the van lurched to the left. The solid ground beneath the tyres turned to gravel, which sprayed up and pinged off the underside of the van.

"This is nuts," Pat whispered to me as we were tossed around. My head slammed against the back of Alma's seat and the bruised lump of flesh there was crushed. I had to grind my teeth together and dig my nails into the sacks to stop myself screaming out loud. Another sharp turn to the left. Pat was caught off-balance and collapsed on top of me with a grunt.

"Crap, sorry!" he yelled as he pushed himself away.

"That's okay. I think you only cracked three of my ribs. I've got plenty others left."

"I'll get 'em next time."

I had my revenge just seconds later, when we swung around yet another bend and I crashed straight into him, somehow managing to head-butt him perfectly in the jaw.

"Sorry guys, hold on," Dad called from the front. We groaned in reply, then were promptly hurled clean off the sacks by a huge bump. We lay there, side-by-side on the dusty floor, with tiny shards of grit and mud flecks stuck in our skin like ice cold pins. The bare metal beneath us vibrated violently. Not quite enough to shake us around, but the tremors caused my spine to itch. If I closed my jaw tight, my teeth actually rattled against each other.

"Can you believe this," Pat said, just loud enough for me to hear over the whine of the engine. "It's like having Jason Statham for a father." His hand pressed over mine, his palm clammy and covered in dust. "What d'you think'll happen if the cops catch us? You reckon we'll go to one of those juvey detention places, young person's institutes or whatever? Like in that film we saw, where those two guards grabbed the weedy bloke with glasses, while he was doing gardening in the prison conservatory? And then they wailed on him, smashing plant pots over his head, just for fun?" He crushed my hand until I thought my knuckles would pop.

"And beat him with their truncheons," I said, the excessive violence still fresh in my mind. Pat had taken great delight in describing every bone-shattering, eye-gouging moment to me in excessive detail while we watched. In fact he really struggled to keep up, as it was pretty much all fighting and violence, and almost no dialogue.

"And stamped on his nuts," Pat said with a shiver.

"Yeah, and wrestled with him."

"Huh?" Pat shuffled beside me. "Wrestled with him?"

"Remember? That bit where the guy was in the showers, then the other prisoners grabbed him and started wrestling with him, bending him about and stuff? He was grunting and screaming, it sounded awful."

"Oh, right, yeah. They were wrestling." He sighed and slammed some part of his anatomy against the floor of the van. "I can't handle it, man." He sounded close to tears. "I don't want to go to prison."

"I'm sure it's not that bad in real life," I lied.

It wasn't until Pat fell silent that I realised we'd slowed to a jerky crawl.

Dad cursed up front, just as the engine spluttered and wheezed, then gave in altogether. We lurched to a sudden and painful halt.

"Right," Dad said. "Everyone out."

"And look, it is starting to rain," Alma said with a sigh. She was right. The gentle tap of raindrops against the roof had swelled to a heavy drumming.

"I'm more worried about the police than a spot of rain. Come on, chop chop!"

The rain itself was surprisingly mild, or at least compared to the freezing gales that whipped through wherever we were stranded. On stepping down from the back of the van, it finally became obvious why the 'road' was so bumpy. It wasn't actually a road at all. The ground was mushy and my feet sank straight in when I jumped down.

"Careful," Alma said. She grabbed my shoulders to keep me steady. "The mud is slippery."

"Mud? Where did we stop?"

"In some sort of field, and God only knows where. I see nothing out here, except for lights from back where we came."

"We're not too far from the carriageway," Dad said as he struggled his way through the mud. As if to prove his point, the distant wail of sirens suddenly cut through the storm from somewhere behind me. There must have been an entire pack of cop cars to make such a loud drone.

The sound made Pat jump.

"Oh crap, you see all those? Are they looking for us? We've gotta get outta here!"

"Relax, they won't spot us out here. By the time they find the van we'll be long gone."

"Won't Davey mind that we left his van out in the middle of some field?" I asked.

"No. He won't mind. Do you guys have a mobile phone, or something with a light on it?"

"Nah, nowt like that."

"Okay, we'll have to make do with our two phones then. Pat, you take my hand, and Alma, you take Joel's. We'll head away from the road, see..."

A blast of icy wind cut out the rest of his sentence, but the next I knew, Alma's hand wrapped around mine and we began our trek through trenches of sludge. The rain stung my cheeks and was fast turning the mud beneath us into glue. Walking was like something out of a terrible nightmare, where your limbs suddenly become leaden and useless. Once my foot had sunk into the filth, it took a concentrated effort to remove it again. Our progress seemed to be no more than a handful of steps a minute.

After quite some time of pulling our way through the muck, the sirens still hadn't faded. In fact, they seemed even louder than before. Pat shouted something across to my left, his words stuttered like machine-gun fire, but I couldn't make out anything he said over the fierce roar of the gales.

The wind suddenly changed direction and pellets of rain fired straight into my face.

"Blagh!" Alma cried out, "this is terrible! Ahh, and now the light goes out! Darrel!"

"The rain must have fried it," Dad called back, his words only just reaching us. "You see that glow over to the left? Let's head towards that!"

"Okay!" We changed direction and staggered towards the light that Dad had spotted in the distance.

I couldn't even begin to guess at how long we spent hacking our way across the torturous swampland. All I know is the rain didn't let off the entire time. Drops the size of marbles bombarded us relentlessly until my skin was raw and slippery and my hair clung to my forehead, glued into place like a plastic wig. Twice Alma stumbled, and both times she dragged me screaming into the mud. The foul muck caked my clothes and invaded my mouth and my nostrils, filling them like cold, slimy fingers. Even after I'd picked myself up and spat on the ground a hundred times, that terrible taste lingered.

"It looks like a farmhouse," Alma shouted when we drew close to the source of the light. By now blasts of thunder swept through the drenched fields, limiting our conversation to the occasional bout of screaming and bellowing.

"What are we going to do when we get there?"

"I think we will find out soon!"

A rough stone wall ringed the farmhouse, but fortunately there was no barbed wire or other deterrents to keep out trespassers. As it turned out, such deterrents were unnecessary anyway. When Dad tried to boost me over the wall, a sliver of fine rock jutting from the top sliced deep into my palm, and I cried out as I lost my balance. I hit the sludge on the other side face-first. I had to kick and writhe to pull myself free of the filth and stagger back to my feet. My hand blazed as dirt invaded the wound. Even with my other hand pressed tight over my injured palm, a drizzle of hot blood slipped through my fingers.

Dad landed next to me with a grunt.

"Joel, bloody hell, are you okay?"

"Yeah," I called back. I shuffled around so he couldn't see me clutching my hand.

"You're sure?" He rested his hand on my shoulder and I thought he was going to twist me around, but then Pat clambered over the wall behind us and encountered the same sliver of rock.

"Waghhh, frigging heck!"

His curses were quickly followed by a splash, and I felt mud bullets bounce off the back of my jeans. Dad let go of my shoulder and stooped to help him up, while I squeezed my injured hand. I tried to focus on the wind that caught against my jacket and lifted it around me like a tattered, mud-soaked sail. Or the icy shower that bit through my clothes and saturated every inch of skin. Anything but the pain.

Another barrage of thunder, almost loud enough to splinter my eardrums, crashed down around us. I have to admit that I ducked slightly, afraid that sheets of lightning would strike down upon us and cook us where we stood. The rain transformed into a sudden lashing of hailstones which rained down like cricket balls. Huge, solid chunks pummelled my scalp until I cried out. I hitched my jacket up to cover my head, but the wind whipped it violently to the side and almost knocked me to the ground for a fourth time.

As soon as Alma was over, she grabbed my hand – good hand, luckily – and we all took off towards the farmhouse.

"Looks like a bedroom light is on upstairs," she shouted between pained squeaks.

"We're not going to knock on their door, are we?" As much as I craved shelter from the weather, I was worried that the family inside might chase us off their land with a shotgun.

"I do not think that is your father's plan."

She was right. We briefly stopped in the blissful partial-shelter at the side of the house. A set of wind chimes pounded out a frantic distress signal over to my right, while an ancient gate that had probably come loose in the storm creaked across to my left. A powerful gust surged past us and the gate slammed shut with such ferocity that I jerked against Alma's grasp. I was sure that the owners would be brought out by the noise. A familiar puddle of tension grew in my gut. The puddle filled my entire stomach when the sound of the slamming gate was accompanied by shattering glass.

"Quick, get in!"

A terrible feeling of déjà vu overcame me as once again I found myself thrown into the back of a car. This time, the seat was high up and covered in some kind of thick, itchy rug. Piles of junk lay on top of the soft fabric, and I tipped the whole lot onto the floor in my flailing attempt to get inside. I scrambled to the far end of the seat, helped along by Pat who crammed his way in after me. Soon, my left shoulder was crushed against a cold steel door.

After a few seconds of hissing and crackling from the front, the engine suddenly kicked in. I was about to question how Dad had managed to get the car started without a key, but I silenced myself. I almost certainly didn't want to hear the answer.

The radio started up a second after the engine. Guess what song was playing.

"Well, I wish it could be Christmas every daaaaaaaaay, oh when the kids start singing and the band begins to plaaaaaaayyyaaay..."

A thin smile stretched across my lips, but the music was immediately cut out by the sound of Alma screaming.

"Someone is coming! Go! Go!"

A tremendous roar shook the entire car. I felt the tyres churn in the mud beneath us, but something was wrong. We weren't moving. The tyres just span aimlessly.

"Go!" Alma screamed again, and she slapped her palms off the dashboard.

"What the hell do you think I'm trying to do!" Dad screamed back. A man slammed himself against the outside of the driver's door and yelled something over the din of the Christmas music.

"... out... thieving... kill you!"

"Bloody hell! Move you fricking piece of junk!"

"He's put a great big smiiiiile on somebody's faaaaayyyyaaaaace..."

The banging stopped and the frantic screams from outside shifted around the front of the car. Alma shrieked again as her door handle rattled. The owner beat his fist against her window and screamed obscenities and from the force of the blows, it was clear he wasn't some elderly fellow who was going to give up his car without a fight.

"Holy crap," Pat said, and he grabbed my arm. "That guy's really pissed off."

"Can you blame him?"

The farmer gave up on Alma's door and moved instead to mine. He pulled on the handle and I could have died right then when the door swung wide open and a freezing blast of rain-soaked wind hit me full in the face, a barrage of ice needles that stung my skin. I was so shocked, I barely had time to gasp before two hands caught me in the chest and grabbed hold of my jacket.

"Gerrout, you frigging gypo!"

"Jesus, let go of him!" Pat screamed.

"...Then your rosy cheeks are gonna light my merry waaaaaaayyyaaayyy..."

Pat clung to my arm but the farmer was strong. I felt myself slip across the seat, towards the biting chill outside. The wheels still churned furiously against the mud, kicking up thick clots that were blown straight into my face by the gales. I gagged and choked, desperate to free myself from the farmer's grasp. My left hand was clamped around the farmer's muscular arm, and I felt the tendons and veins bulge beneath his exposed skin. Meanwhile, my right arm was being wrenched from its socket by Pat. Up front, Alma and Dad screamed – at the farmer, at me, and at each other.

The harder the farmer pulled on my jacket, the further it crept up my body, until one of his hands had slipped to just beneath my jaw. My reaction isn't something I'm proud of, but it was pure survival instinct. I opened my mouth wide and lowered my head, then clamped my teeth around his flesh and bit down. Hard.

The awful Christmas song was suddenly drowned out by the farmer's frantic screams and pleas for me to let go. I hung on like a rabid dog. His skin was tough and hairy. The leathery texture made me gag until spit ran from both corners of my mouth, but still I held on, even when the tips of his hairs tickled my tongue. His other hand pushed against my face to try and prise me away.

"Get your hands off him!" Alma screamed, but she was no longer in the passenger seat. She was outside. The farmer shook as she pelted him with her fists.

"He's biting me! Yaaaggghhhh! The little sod's biting me!"

When I tasted the bitter tang of blood I spat out his hand and a good thing I did too, because Dad threw the car into reverse a second later. This time the entire vehicle shuddered, then lurched backwards. A thud and a cry of pain came from my side, as the open door caught the farmer. Alma continued to yell, but she'd given up assaulting the guy and was chasing after the car instead. Dad pulled to a shaky halt and ground through the gears, which gave her a chance to catch us up and jump back into the passenger seat.

Alma resumed her cries of "go, go, go," and Dad obliged. Both Alma's door and mine slammed shut as we powered forwards through the sludge, before we smashed straight through the creaky gate. Broken pieces of wood were crushed to splinters under the wheels of the car as I clutched a hand to my chest and willed my heart not to burst right there and then.

"Let the beeelllllls ring ouuuut, for Christmaaaaaaaassss!"

Seventeen

I felt horrible as we drove away from the farmhouse. I could still taste the farmer's skin and hear his screams echo around the car. The full realisation of what we'd done slammed home. We were the bad guys here. We'd stolen his car, and most likely left him lying unconscious in the mud outside his home. What if he was still there, face-down in that filth, and there was no one else to help him up and carry him back inside? He could drown out there! Or, at the very least, catch a nasty cold.

The rain and hail continued to assault the roof. My ears ached from the constant bombardment, while my brain did spin cycles every time we hit a dip or a bump in the road. Whatever broken track we were driving down, we had to be the only ones. I couldn't hear any other vehicles over the terrible weather, not even the low rumble of a night lorry. Still, at least the Christmas music had finished. The radio churned out a string of soulless advertisements for cheap toys and winter excursions.

"Escape the holiday blues with a fantastic trip to the Algarve! This December, swap Santa for sangria, and Christmas trees for palm trees! It's our ho-ho-holiday extravaganza, and it ends this weekend at Big Package Travel! *Terms-and-conditions-may-apply-package-includes-hotel-only-and-is-based-on-a-family-of-ten-sharing-a-room-see-our-website-for-details.*"

"Where we gonna go when we leave England?" Pat asked absently, to no one in particular. For a while there was no reply, as if none of us could really think that far ahead.

"Well," Dad said, "we can head wherever you like, but we'd better lay low first. Where do you fancy? Want to escape the holiday blues and head off to the Algarve?"

"Sounds a bit old-personish. Can't we go somewhere fun?"

"Well, I'd better take you boys somewhere safe, first – and Alma, too. We can go somewhere fun later. I've got a brother who lives in California, right on the coast, not too far from Disneyland. Think you'd like that?"

"California? Yeah, that'd be cool. Lots of hot American lasses in bikinis."

"Ahhh," Alma said, laughing. "A man with priorities."

"What do you think, Joel?" Dad asked. "Does America sound good?"

"Won't it take a long time to get there by boat?"

"Ahhh, no rush. We won't go there yet. Maybe head up north first, lay low for a while. Then head for warmer climes."

"I might get a tan," Alma said with a sigh. "First time since I moved to England."

"Hey, don't complain about our weather, babe. I bet you weren't exactly sunning yourself back in Poland."

"In summer we have sunshine, at least. In this country it only rains cats and dogs."

"Ah well, we'll all be in tropical climes soon enough, right lads?"

I nodded and squeezed my hands together, my skin still slippery with mud. Dad was just trying to take our minds off things, I know. It seemed to have worked with Pat, who was already excited about the prospect of cruises and California, but I found that I couldn't relax just yet.

"So is this boat yours?" Pat asked.

"Nope. The boat belongs to Davey."

"Oh, right. I heard him mention it back in the basement. How comes that guy has a boat anyway? He lives in some rundown pub."

"Well," Dad said, "it's not exactly a pleasure ship. It's mostly used for business purposes."

I remembered that conversation back in the basement of the Prince Regent. Something about picking up cargo.

"You ever been on the boat?" Pat asked.

"A few times, but sailing isn't really my thing. Too boring."

"Wait, wait, listen," Alma cut in. "The radio." A gravelly-voiced man with a strange accent read out the latest news report.

"...escaped in a white van. Police are appealing for information..."

The radio cut off and the gravelly tones were replaced with an awkward silence.

We drove like that for what seemed like a long stretch. The constant rain kept me company, tapping a lively beat on my window until Dad finally cleared his throat.

"No one want to talk any more?"

"I always feel sad when it rains like this," Alma said after a beat, her voice hushed.

"How come?"

"Maybe this is not a good time."

"No, go on. It'll take our minds off everything."

"The darkness. The terrible weather. This is just how it was when my grandfather was killed."

The car fell silent again.

"Oh," Dad said, his voice soft. "Maybe you're right. Save that one for another time, eh?"

"Wait," Pat said. He leaned forward in his seat. "I wanna know what happened."

"Well, I will try." She paused to gather her thoughts. "I was just a girl, twelve years, when he died. I lived with my grandfather in a small town above Krakow. He would work until late at the iron mill, and he always took me along so I would not get in trouble without him. I was a quite bad child, you see. When he was at the bathroom, I would sometimes hide one of his tools, and he would always act surprised when he came back, stomping around and scratching his head. He would say it was the mice that stole it, and if he could not find it, I would pretend to find it for him. Then to thank me, he would boost me up on his shoulders. He was so tall, I could see for miles up on top of him." She chuckled, a nervous little laugh that died halfway up her throat.

"One night he finished work and we were driving home from the mill down this…this rocky old road, same way we would always drive. At night there was no lights to show the way. It was raining hard, even worse than now. I have never seen rain so bad. I was terrified the windscreen would smash in on us.

"We were halfway home when it happened. My grandfather could not see a car that had broken down on our side of the road. Not until it was too late. He tried to steer out of the way, but we clipped the bumper and…and we ended up off the road. The next I remember, our car was upside down, and the roof was all bent in and pushing my head to the side. There was a cold liquid dripping across my face. It was all in my eyes. I could not see, and I was so, so scared.

"My grandfather was still stuck in his seat with his seatbelt. I think I was crying. He reached over and squeezed my hand,

and he told me I would be all right. He told me I had to get out, to get back to the road and find help." Her voice was hoarse by now. I shook my head, my lower lip trembling. She had been the same age as me when the accident had happened.

"But I could not leave him. So I stayed in the car. I stayed and held his hand. I sat by his side and listened to his breathing get slow, and quiet, until there was nothing at all." She sniffed, then lapsed into silence.

Pat sat back again without a word.

"Hey, you okay?" Dad whispered to her.

"Yes, I am fine. Sorry, I do not even know why I brought it up. As if we are not already feeling bad enough, right?"

"Don't worry, babe. Soon we'll be on that boat and we can just relax. Well, if we ever find the coast through all this bloody mist."

"Do you know where this road goes?"

"Not exactly. We're still heading east though, as far as I can tell. With a bit of luck, we should be at Ramsgate any time now."

A siren suddenly wailed directly behind us, and my head almost crashed against the roof from the shock.

"No!" Dad shouted from the front. "Not now!" He slammed his hands against the steering wheel. The engine roared as he tortured it, desperate to wring out as much power as possible. Every pothole that we slammed across was like a sideswipe from a rampaging bull. My spine felt like a Jenga tower, ready to collapse into pieces at any moment. But even with the car pushed to its limits, the siren stayed right on our tail.

"Won't be long before more of the sods show up," Dad said. "They'll probably try and head us off."

"Give me the gun," Alma said. Her tone was calm, almost cold.

"What do you want the gun for?"

"Just give it to me, please. Where is it, inside your jacket?" A moment later, I caught the click of the safety being removed. I clutched my seatbelt as Alma's window screeched open. An icy explosion of rainwater caught me full in the face and pressed me back in my seat. I spluttered and turned my head to wipe the freezing drops from my eyes. The roar of the wind through Alma's open window almost matched the whine of the engine, but both were outdone by the terrific blast of gunfire that followed. Behind us, the siren veered to the right and then cut off. Once again we were alone on the road.

"Jesus, that was loud!" Pat shouted. "Did you hit him?" He sliced me with his elbow as he craned around and peered through the rear window. I was too shocked to respond.

"I aimed at the tyre. Not sure if I hit. Maybe I just scared him." She wound the window up again. The bombardment of wind and rain was cut off.

"Well," Dad said, "if they weren't pissed off at us before, they must be by now."

This is just great, I thought. We're officially on the run with Bonnie and Clyde. I imagined us surrounded by police, torn to shreds by endless gunfire. Our bodies dancing on the spot as they spurted gore.

Not long after we pulled onto a smoother road. Once again I could hear sirens, but they sounded distant, and the first bit of good news arrived at last.

"Ramsgate," Dad yelled. He punched the roof and cackled like a madman. "Hah! We found it! Just ten miles to the coast!"

By now it was 3am. It must have been bad enough for Dad

to drive in the pitch black, but that wasn't even the worst of it. Just a mile from the coast, the light mist that clung to the air thickened into a soupy fog. Pat described it as, "Like driving straight into a cloud."

"This is bloody ridiculous," Dad said, wiping frantically at the windscreen.

"At least police might not find us in this," Alma replied.

"Yeah, but it doesn't help us much if I drive this heap straight into the sea, does it?"

Dad eased off the accelerator and my back no longer felt like jelly, but the relief didn't last long. The sirens in the distance were closing in again, trying to beat us to the port. Dad cursed and pushed on as quickly as he dared.

Meanwhile, Pat wriggled constantly in his seat and peered back over his shoulder every few seconds.

"Can you see anything?" I asked, my knees gripped tight.

"Not a thing, man. I can only see a few feet back. Probably won't see 'em till they ram us off the sodding road."

"We've got to make it," I whispered. "We can't come this close and not make it."

Another whoop from Dad, then he gunned the engine.

"There, on the right! We're here!"

We took a mighty swerve to the right then screeched to a halt. Immediately everyone scrambled outside. A hand grabbed me and half-carried, half-dragged me along a row of wooden boards. I could tell it was Alma's hand from the softness of her skin, and the sound of her breathing as we ran.

Our footsteps echoed all around the pier, terrifyingly loud as if we were part of an enormous army mounting an assault. I could only just hear the fierce crashing of the waves against the shore, and the rows of moored boats and ships up ahead, which creaked and strained against their binds. At one point my foot slipped into a gap between the boards and I cried out, sure that it would stay wedged and be torn clean off at the ankle. Alma slowed just long enough for me to work it loose and stagger on.

This was it. Davey's boat was just up ahead, nestled somewhere amongst the others. Our means of escape! For a moment, my hopes were raised. I was certain that we'd made it, that we were on our way to America, to finally make it as a real family.

For just a moment.

Eighteen

I obviously couldn't see the fog, but I could tell it was dense. My skin was drenched in icy moisture within seconds of leaving the warm confines of the car, and every breath felt like a cloud of tiny icicles that pricked my throat on the way down.

I guess it was because of the fog that no one spotted the policeman who stood guard. There was no way he could have missed us, of course. We must have sounded like a startled herd of wild animals, charging straight towards him.

The first I knew he was there was when he mumbled into his radio, just before he called out to us.

"Stop! Hey, stop!" He was directly in front of us.

The shock took Alma off-balance, and the pair of us crashed to the ground for the nth time that night.

"Nnnggg," she wailed as bone collided with solid wood. "My knee!"

"Just stay right there," the cop yelled. He pulled out a set of handcuffs, metal frames that clanged together like the wind chimes back at the farmhouse. I pushed myself up to my knees as Pat and Dad jerked to a standstill.

A second later, I realised the policeman wasn't alone – someone else, another cop surely, strode towards us alongside his partner.

"Back off," Dad said, and the hollow click of the gun's safety pierced the air.

I had just crouched beside Alma, who rocked back and forth across the boards, her leg clutched to her chest. The sound of the gun caused us both to freeze on the spot.

"Okay, okay, okay. Just be calm."

The first cop was clearly the one who did all the talking. The guy sounded petrified, while his partner remained silent. Behind us, the sirens had already blocked off the end of the pier. We were surrounded.

Dad shuffled across to me and Alma. He helped her to her feet, and I rose awkwardly with her.

"Come on," he said. "We've got to go, right now. Pat, take your brother."

Dad handed me off, then walked over to the cops. I could almost imagine the first guy, his hands raised before his face, peering through trembling fingers.

"I'm taking one of you hostage, but I only need one. You."

"You're wasting your time, you know." That was the other cop. Unlike the first guy, there wasn't a hint of fear in his voice.

Dad snorted. "The only one wasting my time is you. You, stop shaking and get down on your knees."

"Why?" asked the first cop. "Why on my knees? God, you're not going to shoot me, are you?" At that moment, I wondered the exact same thing. I didn't realise until Pat winced and pulled back, but I was crushing his hand in my own.

"I said, get down!"

"Dad, just leave him alone!" My free hand had balled into a fist, and my throat burned at the effort. "Let's just find the boat, okay?"

"Okay, Joel. It's okay." He sighed. "Listen, you, down on your knees before I do something stupid." I heard the cop drop from his feet with a whimper. "Good. Stay there and tell the others not to follow us, or your partner tastes a bullet." He turned to us and shouted, "Come on, this way, let's go!"

The second policeman was silent the whole way to the end of the pier. Dad and Alma struggled along just behind him. Pat and me followed at the rear. Just ahead, I could hear Alma's foot drag awkwardly across the wooden boards.

"Crap, this ain't good," Pat whispered, and he crushed my hand in return. "If we don't find this boat, we're trapped here, man."

No problem at all, Dad will find it, was what I wanted to say. But my lips refused to move, as if they were stitched together like some macabre puppet's.

If Dad didn't know where he was going, he sure didn't show it. We twisted right after a few yards and quickly made our way down one of the jetties, not slowing for a moment, not a word said between us.

A sudden gust of wind hurled freezing cold sea spray into my face. I almost choked on the frothy ice water.

"Here," Dad shouted, "this is it! Jump aboard, come on!"

He helped Alma across the narrow gap, Pat and me just a step behind. The hostage was positioned on the other side of the deck. I could tell because his radio blared every few seconds, the disembodied voices of the other cops cutting through the din of the waves that hurled themselves against the boat.

Dad ordered Pat to keep an eye on the cop, but thankfully didn't give my brother the gun, which I'm sure would have elicited a Reservoir Dogs impression. Then he took Alma into the cabin area. A moment later, an engine kicked into life somewhere below my feet and the entire boat trembled.

Pat grabbed my arm to steady me. "D'you think we're gonna take him with us?" he whispered in my ear.

"Who, the cop? I hope not, he doesn't seem too friendly."

"He keeps staring at us. It's creeping me right out. What if he tries to do a runner? What should I do?"

"I don't know, trip him up or something?"

"Assault a copper? Bloody hell, we're gonna be the new Kray twins, aren't we?" His voice cracked apart. "I bet we're gonna be eighty years old, still on the lam, scuttling away from the police on those bloody mobility scooters. It's never gonna end, is it?"

"Hey, you two," the cop hissed at us. "*Listen*, lads. I know you must be in massive shock with everything you've been through, first your mother killed in a fall, then all this running away, now your dad waving that gun about – but he's a dangerous man and this has to stop now, right? You have to get off this boat right now, while you can. Run back down the pier, there's more policemen arriving, they'll take you to safety."

"You mean lock us up," Pat replied tightly, with a sniff. "No, thanks. I'd rather risk it out at sea."

But we were too late. At first, there were voices. They no longer seeped out from the radio, but called through the fog instead. The police were sweeping the area, trying to track us down. Now I could make out footsteps headed our way. Heavy boots thumped across the wooden boards, and the voices grew louder. Just as I was ready to freak out, one of them called:

"Over here! Pier seven!"

I turned, startled by another set of footsteps that crossed the deck towards us. Dad had returned. He shouted to us, his voice calm but commanding.

"Back here, boys! Get away from the edge!"

We did as he said. He grabbed the hostage and the pair of them pushed past us, headed back towards the pier.

"Where are you going?" I asked. Dad stopped for a second,

then stepped back and took my free hand and shoved something into it. Something large and plastic and rectangular. The radio. It squealed, then the crackly, unfamiliar voice of a man hissed out, relaying a bunch of numbers and what sounded like directions.

"Keep a hold of this," Dad said. He patted me on the shoulder. "We can talk over it."

"What do you mean? Where are you going?"

"Don't worry, Joel. I'm not going far."

He climbed back onto the pier with the cop in tow, and left me clutching the radio. I knew I should call to him, but my mouth had dried up. The other cops had surrounded the boat and were yelling at Dad. We could only stand there while it happened.

"Drop the gun, Mr Petersen! We have armed response units on stand by!"

"Get back, will you! Back, right fricking now!"

"Just put the gun down and talk to us. Tell us what's going on here."

"Are you listening to me, you bastards? Back off! Joel, Pat, get inside with Alma!"

I was dragged backwards into the cabin of the boat and Pat slammed the door behind us. Sealed off from the frenzy outside, I slumped against the wall and squeezed the radio. Tears grew behind my eyes, then poured down my cheeks. We were so bloody close. It wasn't fair.

"We must go," Alma said. She sounded angry. Hurt.

"We can't leave," Pat said. "Dad's gone back onto the pier!"

"I know. He showed me how to work the boat."

"What you talking about? He wants us to leave without

him?"

"That is what he told me. We have to go north, follow the coast, he said."

"North where?"

"He said you have an uncle up there, very remote place. We will be safe. Later, we can get help from his contacts, and leave Britain."

"I don't care about that," I shouted. "What about Dad? He's not going to shoot his way off the pier? If he shoots at them, they'll shoot back! They'll kill him!"

"No, he will not shoot. He gave me the bullets."

The radio in my hands silenced us with a frantic hiss, and this time the voice that emerged was immediately familiar.

"Joel, hey, you there? Joel?"

"Dad, hello? Dad?" I fumbled with the radio, searching for some kind of button or switch I could press to respond. Eventually my thumb found a smooth bump and the speaker crackled and fell silent.

"Dad, can you hear me?"

"Hey, there you are. Coming through loud and clear."

"Dad, what are you doing? We can't go without you!"

"You have to, Joel. There's no time to argue, okay?"

"But we came all this way. We only just found you again."

"I know, and I'm glad I finally had the chance to meet you both. I'm just sorry it took so bloody long."

"I don't want to go, if you can't come with us."

"Trust me, it's better this way."

"No, it isn't!" My hands trembled so much that I almost lost my grip on the radio. "You were never going to come, were you? You promised us, but you were never going to come!"

"I'm sorry, Joel. I'm really sorry. I've been breaking

promises all my life. That's why I'm such a useless bloody screw-up. That's why you're all better off without me."

"I don't care if you're a screw-up! I want us to be a family!" The radio hummed then lapsed into silence, but I could hear the police gathering outside. They shouted something, and Dad yelled back.

I shuffled to the door and placed my palm against the freezing cold surface. Pat stepped behind me and gripped my shoulders.

The radio hissed again. "You've already got a family," Dad said. Urgency crept into his voice. "You've got your brother, Joel. And he's so much more than that. He's more of a father to you than I've ever been. Pat, keep on taking care of him for me, you hear?" Behind me, Pat nodded silently. "I love you both, you know that, right?"

"I love you too, Dad." Tears trickled down my cheeks and dripped onto my fingertips.

"Tell Alma I'm sorry, will you? Now go on, get the hell out of here!"

The engine roared and the entire boat jerked backwards, quaking away from the pier. Pat and I fell against the door. The radio fell from my grasp and skidded across the ground, then slammed into the far wall. The crackles and hisses died.

"Hold on to something," Alma said, a little too late.

I pressed my forehead against the door and let the cold seep across my brow. On the other side, the shouting faded.

The boat twisted through the waves and shook from side to side as Alma struggled with the controls. Something scraped against the hull, somewhere deep beneath my feet. We tilted for a moment, then broke away again. Alma muttered something in Polish, desperately trying to turn us around without sinking the whole boat. Pat and I simply clung to whatever we could find and struggled to stay on our feet.

Another collision sent something heavy crashing to the ground across the other side of the cabin. I was sure we'd capsize at any moment and be torn apart by the sea, and I wondered what it would feel like when my lungs filled with slimy sea water.

"Bloody hell," Pat cried out, "watch out!"

"Almost there," Alma shouted back.

By some sort of miracle, we made it out of the port and turned fully around without dying horribly. Now Alma threw us forwards, pointed out to sea. The boat shuddered in place then crept away from the pier, and the voices outside were smothered by the squeal of the engine.

The final traces of Dad had disappeared.

"I can't believe we left him." I shook my head. "I can't believe it."

Pat and Alma said nothing.

Nineteen

I put down my toothbrush and bared my teeth in the mirror, like a savage ready for attack. After a quick gargle, I spat up the froth and wiped my lips with the back of my hand. My tongue tingled with the minty residue.

"Hey, Joel. Did you get the ones at the back?"

That voice! I spun around and gasped.

"Dad?"

"That's right, it's me, son."

"But how did you get away from the cops? And how did you find us out here?"

"Well, you see, there's a very good and simple explanation. I was actually an undercover cop the whole time, infiltrating Davey's gang to bring them all down." He stepped up to me and bent, and his breath warmed my face. "As soon as I explained that to the police on the pier, they apologised and let me borrow one of their fastest speedboats. Fortunately, I'd attached a tracking device to this ship before you guys sailed away, so I was able to chase after you."

"Wow! I just knew you were really an undercover cop!"

"You did? Well, I can't have done a very good job, then!"

He ruffled my head and laughed.

I wrapped my arms tight around him and laughed right along with him. The familiar scent of his deodorant filled my nostrils again. "Oh, I almost forgot. There's someone else who wants to say hello."

A series of excited barks echoed around the tiny cabin. Two warm paws hit me in the stomach and almost bowled me over.

"Chops!"

"That's right. He came bounding up just before I pulled away from the pier. He must've followed you all the way down to London!"

"Oh, wow! It's so good to have you back, boy!" I bent down and scratched at his coat. His tongue smeared a thick coating of molten dog spit across my cheek, but I didn't even care.

"Right, you two come up with me," Dad said.

His hand clamped onto my back and he guided me up the narrow stairs that led from the cabin to the deck. The door creaked open and a glorious burst of sun hit my face.

"Come here, quick!" Alma shouted over the engine's roar. "Time to celebrate!" We joined her near the back of the boat.

"Let's get the party started," Dad said. "I brought us all a pepperoni pizza!"

"That's my favourite!"

"Mine too!" yelled Pat from the door. He bounded up to us and slapped me on the back. "See, Joel? I told you searching for Dad was a great idea!"

"Here's a Dr Pepper for you, Joel." An ice-cold can was slapped into my hand. "Let's enjoy ourselves, eh? Next stop, California!"

"Is this really happening?" I asked as a slice of pizza was dropped into my other hand.

"Well, no," Pat said. "Not really. It's just a dream. But it's a good one, eh?"

"Yeah! Yeah, it's brilliant."

"Come on then, eat your pizza. We've got fifty more to get through back here."

Chops suddenly howled, then leapt at me and knocked me backwards. I staggered away, then flipped over the rails and dropped into the boiling foam of the sea.

Twenty

"Waahhhh!"

I bolted straight up and screamed. My body was trapped under something hot and heavy. I fought as hard as I could, struggling to free myself, until I realised they were just blankets. I was still in bed. My skin was drenched in sweat, which melded the thin fabric of my t-shirt to my skin.

"Joel? That you? Bloody hell's wrong?"

"Pat?" I shook my head and pressed a palm to my chest, which heaved so fast that my ribs ached. "Nothing. Just a dream."

"Nnnnggggg." He shifted in his bed, just a few feet away. A minute later, his snores drifted out from beneath his sheets.

I sat up in bed for a while longer, my knees tucked up to my chin. My brain was far too active for sleep.

"Christmas morning," I whispered to myself. "My first one on a boat."

A short while after, I heard footsteps descend into the cabin. Alma coughed as she sat at the foot of my bed.

"Happy Christmas, Joel."

"Merry Christmas." I stretched, then swung my legs over the edge and hopped onto the bare floor. My toes curled.

"Ugh, cold!"

"I will make us some coffee. Do you think we should wake Pat, too?"

"Maybe later. He'll just be grumpy if we get him up now."

Alma shuffled upstairs and I perched on the edge of my mattress, my hands clasped in my lap. My brother and I had barely talked as we headed out to sea after leaving the pier. Alma had been silent too, aside from the occasional grunt or curse as she mulled over the boat's controls. I'd battled with the radio, trying to get anything but static out of it, and failing miserably.

Later, Alma sorted out a delicious festive dinner with the occasional bit of help from me. She said it was 'the Polish custom to have feast and presents,' and I wasn't going to argue.

Pat showered and joined us back upstairs when we called him, collapsing with a sigh on the plastic bench.

"You guys get me any good presents, then?" he asked.

"Yes." I smiled and nodded. "We made a tree."

"A tree? Where is it?"

"Right here," Alma said.

Pat giggled. "Call that a tree?"

"Why?" Alma said. "What is wrong with our tree?"

"It's a bit of seaweed wrapped round a pencil."

"There was not much more seaweed around for us to use. Could you find any better at sea?"

"Nah, probably not, in five minutes." He let out a tremendous belch, which I could practically smell from the other end of the cabin. "What we got for Christmas dinner, then? I'm starving."

"Baked beans," I muttered. "Christmas baked beans."

"Aw no, I hate beans. Isn't there owt else?"

"Nice spam," Alma said, full of enthusiasm. "For the second course. And we also have tinned peaches for dessert."

"Bloody beans and spam. This boat's going to smell rotten, man."

I grinned toward Alma.

Despite his protests, we served up the beans and slices of jelly meat and sat around the tree for our festive meal. I didn't mind so much that the food wasn't great, and there were no presents or crackers or anything. I still had Dad at the back of my mind, but this was already ten times better than any Christmas we'd had back home.

"What should we do now?" Alma asked when we'd finished.

"Pin the tail on the donkey?" Pat suggested. "We don't even need a blindfold, if Joel goes first."

"But we don't have a tail, or a donkey," I said.

"I could sing, if you like?" Alma suggested.

I nodded. "Yeah, that sounds good. What can you sing?"

"Well, what would you like?"

"How about some Bob Marley?"

Pat snorted. "Very Christmassy, that is."

"I can sing Bob Marley," Alma said. She ruffled my hair, cleared her throat, then burst into a rendition of 'Stir It Up'.

I lay back across the floor and rested my head in my hands. Her voice was beautiful. The song was beautiful too, just as Laura promised as we'd waited at that bus stop – was that really just a day or two ago? My mind drifted, and I felt myself slipping into a peaceful, contented sleep.

A little while later I woke, hard and sore from the deck boards.

"You've been asleep a couple of hours," Pat said, helping me to my feet and slapping me on my back. "Come on, let's head inside."

I staggered across the deck, where the waves lashed us with freezing sea water. The night seemed vast as it sounded out around us, our boat nothing more than a tiny speck in its middle.

Pat led me down to the cabin, but while he collapsed into a blusterous sleep at once, I lay on my bunk shivering under a pile of blankets. My mind churned, despite every attempt to silence it. I began to replay the pier scene over and over in my head. I tried to find a scenario where Dad wasn't left behind, surrounded by cops, and we all managed to take off together. Everything I tried seemed to end up worse – Dad blasted apart by bullets, or all four of us surrounded out at sea by pirates and smashed by cannonballs or whatever. It was like my brain was allergic to happy endings.

On my fifth or sixth re-run of what had happened, I was standing with Pat on the deck of the boat, with the hostage cop on the opposite side. This time *Pat* had the gun, for rather hazy reasons. He had it trained on the cop, who was going through his 'Listen, lads' routine.

"*Listen*, lads. I know you must be in massive shock with everything you've been through, first your mother killed in a fall, then all this running away, now your dad waving that gun about – but he's a dangerous man and this has to stop now, right? You've got to get off this boat, while you can. Run back down the pier… "

"Shut the frig up, copper!" Pat screamed, and my ears exploded as he fired round after round into the unfortunate cop. Pat's hysterical laughter could barely be heard over the din of the cracking gun, although the cop's screams were rather – musical –

"Wait! What did you say?"

The shots ended, and I threw myself across the deck and found the cop's body, limp and slick with blood. I supported his head as he hacked and coughed, and something wet sprayed across my wrist.

"Uggh. I was just saying, ugh, he's a…ungh…dangerous man. He –"

"No, no, before that! The bit about how we've been through a lot!"

"Oh, right. Sorry." He sat up and said, "*Listen*, lads. I know you must have had a massive shock, your mother killed in a fall, then all this running away, your dad waving that gun about – but he's a dangerous man and this has to stop now, right? You have to get off this boat right now, while you can. Run back down the pier…" I let out a shrill laugh and jumped to my feet. The cop's head smacked back onto the deck.

A second later I was standing over Pat in his bed, my hands clamped to his shoulders. I shook him with all my might.

"Holy bloody bastard sodding hell! What you doing, you little – "

"Shut up, listen to me!"

I released him and caught my breath. "Do you remember what that cop said to us back on the deck before we sailed off?"

"What? Yeah, he told us to run off the boat and go and see his copper mates, like I was falling for that one."

"But before that, remember? He said we must be in shock with everything we'd been through, and then he said 'our mother killed in a fall'. You *see*?" From his grunt it was clear he didn't see, and he'd rather I shut up and left him to sleep. "Our mother killed in a *fall. Why would he say that if she'd died from being smothered?*"

"Wait – wh – what?" The cogs kicked into motion, and a few seconds was all it took. "Holy crap, you're right! He said *fall!* So…what…? She was already dead when I…" He huffed and pushed his way out from the covers. "But what about her mouth? I saw her lips move."

"But that would've been a twitch! That's what happens when people die, right? Remember that movie, 'No Guts, No Gory', where the guy had his head bashed in with a crowbar? You said his body was jiggling about the place for *ages* after." I felt terrible comparing our mother to a character in a horror movie, but it was the best example I could come up with.

"Bloody hell. Oh, man…it was an accident…?"

"So now we can stop running. We can go back," I said. Pat seemed to be holding his breath. I went on, blurting out facts that suddenly struck me. "And – listen, Pat, we wrapped her in that Winnie-the-pooh blanket, and – and you tried to revive her! They must have found that, found evidence you did that."

"I never thought of that." Pat's voice was thick. "But… what if the copper was lying, and it's some sort of trap or summat?"

"No, it's not a trap, Pat. I could tell he was telling the truth. He had no idea you thought you'd killed her. Besides, I always thought it was strange how you could have killed her. I was there, and it was all so fast – you can't even smother someone that fast in the movies."

Pat sat up and swung his legs over the side of the bed.

"We didn't do anything wrong," I went on. "And if we go back now we can help Dad out. Be together with him again."

"I dunno if we should go back, man. He told us not to."

"But he didn't know that you didn't kill her. Come on, this is our chance to sort it out for him." I kicked Pat's leg. "Do you really think we'd make it to Scotland on this thing, anyway?"

"But…" He sighed and kicked me back. "But what will we say? What if it doesn't work out?"

"It will." I don't know how, I just knew it. "Listen, if we go back now, we'll – we'll be the lost boys returning from the dead, recovering from our – *psychological trauma.* They might say Dad was kidnapping us, maybe even try to say he came to the house and pushed Mum and took us away, but he can prove that's not true, and we can tell them the truth, say we were in a panic after she tripped and died, and then after we found him, he was just protecting us so we wouldn't be split up because he's not a fit father and we ran away after an accident."

I smiled, and I could tell that Pat was smiling, too.

"Yeah," he said. "And he *was* just protecting us. It's true. Like a hero or someone."

"Yes, like a famous hero or someone like that – "

"And – hey!" Pat said quickly, "we might even be famous, too! We might get fit lasses coming up to us in the street, wanting to ask us for our autographs – "

"Yeah, and I can sign mine in braille!"

We threw on our jackets, then charged upstairs, shouting, "Alma!" "Alma!"

"Listen – Dad – he didn't do it, I mean, Pat didn't do it!" "I didn't – we have to go back!" "It was an accident!" "We can tell them!" "She tripped over the rug!"

"Hey, hey, slow down," Alma said. She wrapped a muffler around my head. "Okay. One at a time, now. Tell me everything."

Five minutes later, we ran out of words and stood in front of her, puffing and panting.

"So that's it," Pat said. I gasped in agreement.

Alma let out a deep breath, then she reached out her arms and wrapped us both in a huge hug.

"This is right," she whispered. "Yes, it is. And Joel…you're a little genius."

She turned back to the wheel, and we huddled close to her as the boat began a slow loop round.

I took Pat's hand, and felt Alma grab my other. Together we stood at the helm of the boat and waited.

Somewhere, off in the distance, I was sure I heard a string of excited barks.

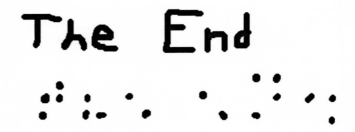

9 781905 796250